W9-BZG-100

COOL FOR THE SUMMER

Also by Dahlia Adler

NOVELS

Behind the Scenes

Under the Lights

Just Visiting

Last Will and Testament

Right of First Refusal

Out on Good Behavior

ANTHOLOGIES (AS EDITOR)

His Hideous Heart: 13 of Edgar Allan Poe's Most Unsettling Tales Reimagined

That Way Madness Lies: 15 of Shakespeare's Most Notable Works Reimagined

C♥♥L

for the
Summer

DAHLIA ADLER

W

WEDNESDAY BOOKS
NEW YORK

First published in the United States by Wednesday Books, an imprint of St. Martin's Publishing Group

www.wednesdaybooks.com

Library of Congress Cataloging-in-Publication Data

Names: Adler, Dahlia, author.
Title: Cool for the summer / Dahlia Adler.
Description: First edition. | New York : Wednesday Books, 2021. | Audience: Ages 14-18. |
Identifiers: LCCN 2020053234 | ISBN 9781250765826 (hardcover) | ISBN 9781250765833 (ebook)
Subjects: CYAC: Dating (Social customs)—Fiction. | High schools—Fiction. | Schools—Fiction. | Bisexuality—Fiction.
Classification: LCC PZ7.1.A25 Coo 2021 | DDC [Fic]—dc23
LC record available at https://lccn.loc.gov/2020053234

Our books may be purchased in bulk for promotional, educational, or business use. Please contact your local bookseller or the Macmillan Corporate and Premium Sales Department at 1-800-221-7945, extension 5442, or by email at MacmillanSpecialMarkets@macmillan.com.

First Edition: 2021

10 9 8 7 6 5 4 3 2 1

To Tamar—
This may not be a "sister" book,
but what fiction could compare to the real thing anyway?

COOL FOR THE SUMMER

Chapter One

NOW

All things considered, high school's been pretty good to me. Granted, if ever I get too whiny about anything, my mother will start comparing my woes of not having my own car to *her* woes of not having her own shoes growing up in Russia, but even in my worst moments of spoiled bratdom, I know that having good friends, decent grades, frequent party invites, and perpetually clear skin makes me one of the luckiest of the lucky.

Sure, my dad's a disappearing shithead and I didn't get the pony I wanted for my ninth birthday, but overall, I'd say life's delivered pretty nicely.

So why is it, when I walk into Stratford High on the first day of senior year, I am immediately reminded of what I don't have? Why must all six feet three inches of Chase Harding, unreciprocated love of my life, be the very first person I see? Why must he be right down the hall from the school's entrance, cracking up guys from the football team, stupid-hot calves on blatant display of stupid-hotness?

How dare, universe. How dare.

"Watch that drool, Rissy. Someone might slip."

"I was hoping you would," I reply without shifting my gaze one iota. I don't need to look up to know that Shannon Salter is speaking. She's the only one who'd dare to call me Rissy. The only one who could without taking my gel manicure to the eyeball, really.

Still, after another beat, I turn away. Even I know I'm bordering on pathetic.

"I missed you, you bitch," Shannon says, pecking my cheek. "I hate your tan."

"You wish you had my tan."

"Of course I wish I had your tan." Shannon winds one of my shoulder-dusting butter-colored curls around her index finger and tugs. "And look how cute this haircut is! And how blond! How dare you spend the summer at the beach without me."

"You were literally in Paris, Shan."

"Oh right, I was." She smiles widely enough to make dimples pop on her peaches-and-cream-skinned cheeks. "Shit, I am cool."

She is, unfortunately. Even during this brief conversation, randos have dropped little "Hey, guys" in our direction, but mostly it's "Hi, Shannon!" with a wave or a smile, careful not to disturb our post-summer reunion, but eager to start the year off right by cozying up to the most popular girl at Stratford.

As if Shannon's desperate for new friends.

It was weird spending the entire summer apart. We haven't done that in years, and certainly not since high school began. But then, my mom had never been asked to accompany her boss to the Outer Banks for the summer. And she'd never dragged her daughter with her, rather than let her stay home alone in Stratford.

It was a summer of firsts.

"So cool," I confirm, giving her a smooch on the cheek that leaves a coral lip print. "And we're reunited, so that's what's—"

"Hey, ladies."

The greeting isn't a tentative drive-by like the others, and it comes complete with a shadow. A six-foot-three shadow. I am not the squeeing type, but if I were, I'd be shattering some eardrums. "Hey, Harding." Do I sound too flirty? I might sound too flirty. But the way he's leaning against my locker is definitely flirty, so really, I'm not being weird. "Did you get taller over the summer?"

Okay, now I'm being weird.

"I did, thank you for noticing." He squints at me like he's scrutinizing my face. "You look different too, Bogdan."

"In a good way?"

He flashes me a smile, revealing the crooked teeth that only make him cuter. "In a very good way."

"That's what I was just telling her," says Shannon, looping an arm around my shoulders. "Look at this hot bitch."

"I am, I am," Chase says with a grin, but I barely hear him. A ghost is walking through the door of the school. A ghost with smooth bronze skin and full lips and lush dark waves and amber eyes that I know from experience can convince you to do things you never, ever dreamed you would.

Things you liked. Things you loved. Things you've thought about with the lights off every night since.

Why is there a Jasmine Killary–shaped ghost haunting Stratford?

Haunting me?

"Yo. Bogdan." Meticulously manicured nails snap in front of my face. "Where'd you go?"

I blink, expecting my vision to clear, but Jasmine's still there, a flesh-and-blood being whose face may be partially obscured by a phone, but whose very real existence is as undeniable as the thunderous pounding in my chest at the sight of her.

Where'd you go?

How do I tell my best friend I don't even know where to begin answering that question?

THEN

The air is different in the Outer Banks, but then, everything is. The houses are all elevated on slats of wood to prevent destruction by flooding. The main road spanning southward from Sea Level is wide and flat and lonely. Nothing is more than two or three stories, tops. It's a far cry from the suburbs of New York City and the summer I am supposed to be spending hand-selling books, consuming my weight in frozen yogurt, babysitting the Sullivan triplets, and glaring jealously at

Instagram selfies of Shannon posted from the top of the Eiffel Tower.

It wasn't a dream summer plan, but it was mine, wrecked the instant my mom swept into our apartment and announced I had a week to pack an entire summer's worth of stuff. I wasn't happy about it—any of it—but I'm not eighteen yet and I can't exactly show up at my dad's house for the first time in years, begging to be babysat. Instead, I spent a week moping in front of crappy TV, said goodbye to my friends, packed my duffel bag with clothing meant for moping, and we were off.

It's a little humiliating staying in the guest suite of my mom's boss's huge beach house, but at least it has a small second bedroom for me with an incredible view of the Atlantic. Declan Killary, CEO of Decker Industries, either did something very right in a past life, or does a lot of terrible shit in this one.

It only takes half an hour for us to get settled before we're summoned to the kitchen—or at least my mother is. I tag along because what on earth else am I supposed to do?

Plus, I'm hungry.

Thankfully, Mr. Killary is generous with the contents of his fridge, basically telling me to go to town before turning to my mom for the rundown of his schedule for the night. You'd think it'd be pretty chill, given he's at his vacation house, but by the time I tune out in favor of celery and peanut butter, he's already been advised of three conference calls, given a set of renovation plans to review for his Dallas office, and told he has a date at 10:00 p.m. at a wine bar in Kill Devil Hills. I pretend not to hear the last part. It's gotta be embarrassing for a seventeen-year-old to overhear that your secretary makes your romantic social plans, but if he's noticed I'm still in the room, there's no indication.

I concentrate extra hard on picking up as much peanut butter as possible.

They're going over tomorrow morning's schedule when a whirlwind sweeps into the kitchen in a blur of long black curls and longer tanned legs. It whooshes right past me to the fridge, nearly whacks me with the door as it pulls out a coconut water, and lets out a moan loud enough to shake the walls as it—she—takes a long sip.

I'd think she hadn't noticed anyone in the room at all, but then she complains, "It is so fucking hot outside. I need to jump in the pool." And then she looks right at me with the closest thing to golden eyes I've ever seen. "Who are you?"

"Manners, Jasmine," says Mr. Killary. "You remember my assistant, Anya?" He gestures to my mom, who looks completely unfazed. "This is her daughter, Larissa. They're staying with us this summer. Didn't your mother tell you?"

She shrugs. "I might've been tuning her out at the time." At least she's honest. "You have a bathing suit?" she asks me.

I do, though I have a feeling it cost about five hundred dollars less than whatever Jasmine's about to put on. "Yeah."

"Great. Let's go." She walks out of the kitchen, coconut water in hand, leaving me no choice but to follow.

I kind of hate her on sight. You can tell she's the kind of girl who always gets what she wants. And she makes me hate myself a little too, because I'll be as susceptible as everyone else who wants to make her happy. You don't spend three years as Shannon Salter's right-hand girl without learning how to spot these personalities faster than you'd spot the perfect jeans at Nordstrom Rack, and it never gets less annoying to make their acquaintance.

I love Shannon, but I get enough of being second place during the school year. I really don't need to spend my summer that way too.

But a pool is a pool and if I'm going to be stuck here all summer, I'm sure as hell gonna get an epic tan.

It takes me longer than it should to choose between my favorite gingham bikini and a hotter but more boring pink one—do I want to show off my fashion sense, or my genetically blessed waist?—and I end up going with the former. Of course, Jasmine wears a tiny patterned metallic thing that's infinitely cooler than mine and shows off a body with both curves and muscle tone, because that's what her kind does. I just sigh and dive in.

To her credit, she doesn't try and chat with me too much. There's no session of picking the interloper's brain and assessing their threat level. So maybe she isn't exactly Shannon. She even whips out an actual novel, which Shannon would never, ever do.

I don't know how to feel about this.

Before I know it, I'm the one making conversation.

"Reading for school?"

Her eyes stay on the page, but she lifts the book enough for me to see she's definitely not doing a summer reading assignment, unless she goes to an extremely liberal school that assigns graphic novels instead of classics by dead white guys. Which she might, since she's outclassing me on everything else.

"Cool. I read for fun too." Did I actually say that? Please tell me I did not say that. Next thing I'm going to be pouring my heart out about my five hundred deleted attempts at writing a romance novel. "I didn't even know your dad had kids," I continue, hating myself for babbling while Jasmine makes it clear she's not interested in conversation.

"Kid." She tilts her face up at the sun, glare reflecting off the shades of her designer sunglasses. "Just me. I live with my mom in Asheville. You did know he was divorced, didn't you? Or did you think your mom was banging a married man?"

Lordy, she is a Type. But I am used to Types. I can handle Types. "I did know, and they're not banging. But if you're looking for a partner in crime for a *Parent Trap*–style summer, you're out of luck."

Her perfect white teeth flash in a smile. "God, I can't imagine anything worse." She sits up and I think she's looking at me, but it's impossible to tell through her mirrored aviators. "I'll take a designated driver for a party tonight, though. It'll be a good one. I promise."

Inviting me to the pool and a party in the first hour we meet? Either Jasmine is way more of a people person than she lets on, or she's really lonely. It doesn't really matter. I know nobody here and have no choice but to accept the invitation.

But here's the thing I learned about Jasmine that day: her promises are always, always for real.

Chapter Two

NOW

I'd extricated myself from my conversation with Shannon and Chase with mumbled excuses earlier, but by the time I slide into my seat behind him in my second period calculus class after fruitlessly spending first period history scouring every corner of social media for clues as to what the hell Jasmine is doing here, I'm determined to shove her out of my mind and get my shameless flirt on.

Apparently, so is he.

"Yo, you coming to my game Friday night?" His face is turned just enough for me to be sure he's talking to me, his right dimple displayed in its full glory. I have dreams of doing weird things to those dimples.

"We'll see." As a rule, I limit how many football games I go to in a season. It's a little too sad to spend all my time drooling over Chase and his magical shoulders. (Or watching him wipe his face on his jersey, revealing his lickable abs. Or making up odes to his butt.) And I certainly don't need him to know how happily I'd give up any night to watch him play. Shannon put me on a strict limit of two games a month, and I've found it to be a good rule. "We might go to Kiki's—gotta get in all the night swimming possible while the weather's still good."

Translation: I am not that interested in you and I'd sooner hang out with the same girls I do all day, every day, and also, I'll be in a bikini.

"So, you'll be in a bikini."

I smile sweetly. "I guess that's possible."

"Suddenly I don't wanna go to my game either." That dimple appears again, and he turns and faces forward as Mr. Howard calls everyone to attention.

Okay, what the fuck is happening? I've spent three years of high school trying to get Chase's attention, and that's after God knows how many years of middle school when I never even bothered to try. And now he's just . . . giving it up.

I really should've given a bigger tip for this haircut.

While Mr. Howard introduces himself for those who don't know him (he taught me in freshman algebra), I slide my phone under my desk and open my ever-running group text with Shannon, Kiki Takayama, and Gia Peretti. *Pool @ Kiki's Fri night? Just us?*

Shannon writes back almost immediately. *Are you seriously pretending you don't wanna go to Chase's game on Fri?*

Then, *Good girl.*

I have to go, Gia reminds us, followed by a megaphone

emoji which, fair, seeing as she's head cheerleader. When we were on the JV squad together freshman and sophomore year, we got reamed out if we missed games for anything short of an emergency. (Aaaand that's why only one of us continued on to varsity.) Not that Gia would've skipped for anything short of landing in a full-body cast. The only thing that girl loves more than cheerleading is being a girlfriend. *What about Hunter's?*

Missing Hunter Ferris's annual First Party does seem like Stratford sacrilege, but come to think of it, I haven't heard a word about it all day. His stupid posts about cabinets full of booze and the majesty of his hot tub usually take up my entire feed.

He's not doing it this year, says Shannon, and I can feel her smugness through my phone screen at already having the dirt. Of course she withheld it. Of course she did. And then she drops another bomb. *Some new girl is.*

Jasmine. I know it in my bones. It's such a Her thing to do, to swoop in and fuck things up a little just because she can. She wants to give the impression that nothing fazes her. And admittedly, very little does, as far as I can tell. Which is annoyingly compelling.

Almost as annoyingly compelling as being allowed to see what *does* get to her.

Stop, I order my quickening pulse as Gia responds with a shocked-face emoji.

I hate lying to my friends, especially after years of them holding my hands through my Chase obsession, but there's no way I can tell them about Jasmine. What would I even say? How do you tell people who've listened to you babble about your crush on a guy for a thousand years that whoops, you spent the summer fooling around with a girl? Especially if you have no idea what it meant to either of you? *Especially* if she's so clearly over it that she came to your school and didn't give you a heads-up?

The only thing I can do is feign complete ignorance and try to keep her far, far away from them.

We're not going to some rando's house, are we? I type, knowing I have no shot at winning this.

Are you joking? Recon 101. There's nothing Kiki loves more than high school espionage. She wants to be either a PI or an investigative journalist, depending on the day. *We're going.*

Even knowing it was coming, my pulse races at the thought of all of us walking into this party together. Immediately, I try to imagine what my friends will think of her.

Ever the detective, Kiki will dig into what possibly could have brought her here for senior year, and I can't blame her—I'm dying to know the same. We spent the entire summer together and she never once said a word about anything other than going home to her mom's in Asheville. How could she not have told me she was moving in with her dad? How could she not tell me that the last time we said goodbye wasn't the last time at all? How could she show up and expect me not to obsess over what it means??

It wouldn't be the worst thing if Kiki got some answers.

As for Shannon, she won't like Jasmine. Outside of our little group, Shannon doesn't really like anybody.

Some days I'm not even sure she likes me. But Jasmine's hot and rich enough to ping Shannon's "importance" radar, so she'll at least pretend to be friendly and welcoming until she figures out whether Jasmine's a threat to her popularity, or college prospects, or both. Basically, whatever dirt Kiki doesn't get, Shannon will. I probably need to figure out how to keep them apart until graduation day.

Gia will spend the entire night trying to decide if Jasmine's prettier than her. She is, but Gia will pretend not to come to this conclusion, while coming to this exact conclusion. I love that she always tries to wish her truths into existence. It isn't that she's lying; it's that she truly believes that if you will it, it is no dream. Her ex-boyfriend taught her that one, though I'm sure she thinks he made it up and doesn't realize it's a famous quote he must've stolen from an old yearbook. Anyway, it's become her strategy for life. Granted, she made cheer captain, has a cute boyfriend who's hopelessly devoted to her, and obviously has the most fabulous friends at Stratford, so maybe she's on to something.

I'd never tell her this, but I was inspired enough by her success to try it with Chase, spending nights willing him to offer me a ride home or ask me to dance at a party. As I think about him flirting with me this morning, I wonder if it's finally paying off, but on delay. (Oh, the timing.)

He'll be at the party; the football players always go, regardless of their opener results. Whether I'm there or not, he and Jasmine will be in the same room, like worlds colliding. I wonder if he'll think she's pretty. (How can he not?) I wonder if she'll think he's hot. (How can she not?) *Did I mention him to her?* I can't seem to recall any conversations about him, but there's no way I went the entire summer without any. Then again, he was oddly unimportant when I was around her. But he's definitely not unimportant now.

The problem is, neither is she.

Ugh, what a mess.

There's a loud coughing sound at the front of the room and I see Mr. Howard trying to get my attention. Frankly, it's perfect timing, so I slide my phone back in my bag without complaint and focus on the word "calculus" glaring at me in red from the whiteboard.

Within minutes my focus is gone. Jasmine isn't in this class, and she wasn't in my first period history class either. What's she taking? Is she in AP Calc, like Kiki? Is she in the other calculus section with Shan and Gia? She wasn't in lab with me and she's not with me now and she won't be in my Spanish class because she's fluent in French.

Who. The fuck. Cares. I am not Jasmine Killary's keeper. I'm not even Jasmine Killary's friend. If I were, I'd have known she was coming here. I'd know why custody changed hands and when she arrived, and we'd have driven to school together the same way we went everywhere together this summer.

Instead, all I know is we haven't spoken since I left the Outer Banks, and maybe it's best we keep it that way.

I fix my gaze on the back of Chase's head, remembering how flirty he was this morning. *That* is where my mind should be.

A note falls on my desk a couple of minutes later, crumpled and ink-smudged. "You should reconsider Friday night," it says. "I could use a personal cheerleader."

I stare at the handwriting I wish I didn't know so well, considering it's the first note Chase has ever sent me that wasn't asking for homework. What does it even mean? Does he remember that I used to be a cheerleader, standing on the sidelines in a tiny top and even tinier skirt? Or does he think I'm so into him I'll cheer him on no matter what? Or is it just him flirting?

Ugh, I might've liked it better when he treated me like his little sister. Romantic intrigue isn't my forte; why would it be when my heart's been in the same unrequited place forever? Not that I haven't dated or made out with guys or anything—and this summer was something else entirely—but it was all fun and games, flirting and having company alongside Gia and Tommy and Shannon and "Pick of the Month." Chase was always real, too real, but also not real at all.

I debate not writing back, but who am I kidding? "I'll think about it."

Even with my eyes on the board, I can see his smug smile in perfect detail after he unfolds my note.

I don't hate it.

As predicted, I don't have a single class with Jasmine that morning, and there's no spotting her at lunch, since Shannon promptly sweeps me, Gia, and Kiki into her car to take advantage of our first day of senior privileges by eating off campus. I do get to hear plenty about her, though, since everyone else has seen her, and they have lots and lots of opinions.

"She moved here from Asheville, North Carolina," says Kiki, her hands flailing like they do when she's excited about info she's uncovered, sleek black-painted fingernails catching the light at Lily's Café. "Her mom's still there, but Jasmine's living with her dad now. Apparently he's some big CEO and his house is incredible."

"Who knew they had Balenciaga out in the sticks?" Shannon stabs methodically at a lettuce leaf. She always eats as if she's dissecting a lab rat.

"What's with her hosting the party?" Gia asks.

"Rumor has it, Hunter tried working his charm on her with a party invite and she looked right at him and said she was busy that night with her housewarming and he was welcome to come. By next period, he was telling everyone the party had moved." Kiki is a fount of information, barely stopping to inhale her pizza. Except none of it is the information I care most about, like *why* she's living with her dad now and *why* she didn't tell me she was moving here, but I'm thirsty for any and all of it and I'll take what I can get.

I listen silently as my three best friends break down everything from Jasmine's wardrobe (expensive) to her hair (too long, Gia thinks, and I shove three fries in my mouth at once so I don't say a word about how she wouldn't think that if she'd ever wrapped it around her fingers) to her flawless French (which I can attest is panty-droppingly good).

Jasmine was supposed to be my secret, and in one morning, she's become the world's top news story.

I really need to change the subject.

"I can't believe we're still talking about this girl when

Chase Harding has been hitting on me all morning," I say with an aggrieved sigh, and though I meant it as a subject-changer, I'm also a little disappointed. I've made these three girls sit through hours upon hours of Chase obsession, and the morning he returns the slightest bit of interest, there's no parade in my honor? What the hell, ladies? How am I supposed to process this on my own?

"I thought we were playing it cool," says Shannon, smirking like she's trapped me in something. "So much for that, I guess."

"What does that mean?"

"He told Alex you're playing hard to get," says Kiki, helping herself to my fries. "Said you gave him a big ol' 'maybe' about the game Friday night."

"But you *are* going, right?" Gia asks, starting to follow Kiki's lead with my fries before yanking her hand back as she presumably remembers it's cheer season. "You guys promised you'd come watch me."

We did? Shit. So much for playing hard to get. "Of course we're going," Shannon says before I can get in a word. "Riss is just making Chase sweat."

"We'll be there," I promise Gia, and Kiki nods in agreement.

"And after, we'll all go to New Girl's party," Kiki adds. Like that, the conversation returns to Jasmine, and I contemplate whether one can literally drown herself in ketchup.

It isn't until last period—English, because of course it would be our shared favorite subject—that I finally have a Jasmine sighting. She slips in right as the bell rings, giving me no chance to make eye contact. I don't even know if she sees me. But it's unmistakably her and her jangling bracelets and her smoky voice saying "Here" and God, I can't even remember what class this is anymore.

She doesn't say another word for the rest of it, and neither do I, but I pack up slowly, sure she'll saunter over on her way out—maybe with a "Hey, Tinkerbell." Heat rises in my cheeks as I imagine it, and I take my sweet time getting my stuff into my bag, waiting for the scent of her favorite peach body lotion to reach me. When I finally can't take it anymore, I look up . . . and the room is empty.

Okay, what the fuck? Even if she didn't see me when she came in, she has to have heard me respond to "Bogdan, Larissa" during roll call. I'm not letting her ignore me. A few weeks ago, we were staying up all night watching movies with our legs intertwined in the dark, tasting the salty-sweet of popcorn mixed with M&Ms on each other's lips, and now . . . this? What even is this?

I have to storm all the way outside before I catch up to her, but there she is, getting into the Jeep I know better than my mom's old Toyota. "Jasmine!"

She pauses. Steps out of the car. Slowly. Like she knew this was coming and has been dreading it all day. She doesn't say a word, just waits. It's her thing—she's chased, never chases. I'd thought I was exempt. "Jasmine," I repeat when I'm standing a few feet away, like I still need to confirm.

"Larissa."

Not Tinkerbell, not a sing-song accented "Larotchka" to affectionately mimic my mom. Just . . . Larissa.

"What are you doing here? Why didn't you tell me you were moving?" I feel silly asking the most basic questions, but I don't know what else to say.

She shrugs. "We weren't really talking anymore when my parents decided, so."

"Okay, but we weren't talking because—" The words burst from my lips and stop. We weren't talking because it was too damn hard after the intensity of that summer. I tried so many times, but my hands would always shake as I typed and erased, typed and erased. It was too impossible to reduce our communication to texts or even phone calls, and I didn't know what to say, how to start. So, I didn't, and neither did she.

"But you're here" is all I manage. *Don't you want to be friends?* hangs in the air in front of my lips. But I can't seem to give it voice, because "friends" doesn't feel like the right word for what we were. Being something else here, in Stratford, away from the magic of the Carolina coast, around Shannon and Chase and real life . . . none of it makes sense.

"Right, I am, and I'm the one who has to meet new people and shit, so." She tugs on the familiar gold necklace hanging at her throat, the hamsah and six-pointed star charms clinking against each other quietly. "Role reversal."

"You already know one person," I point out. "That's one more than I knew."

"Well, when I walked in, the one person I know was otherwise occupied," she says casually, and I realize she's talking about watching me flirt with Chase in the hallway. It feels like a little punch to the gut, knowing that was her "welcome" to Stratford, and I feel like I should apologize, but . . . for what?

"You could've interrupted."

"You and the legendary Chase Harding? I would never."

The words suggest she's hurt or mad or maybe both, but her tone doesn't suggest either one. If anything, it sounds like she's in on a joke.

How do I respond to that?

"Anyway, turns out I don't even need to know you to get a party invite, so."

"I heard. And apparently you're the person to go to for an invite now."

Her full lips, uncharacteristically bare and lightly chapped, curve into a smile. "I suppose I am."

"So," I ask, genuinely unsure, "do I make the cut for your inaugural Stratford party?"

She slips into her car then, taking a seat behind the wheel and closing the door, although the window is wide open. "I'll think about it."

Chapter Three

"You didn't tell me Jasmine was moving here," I say accusingly to my mother the second she walks into the kitchen after a day spent taking messages for my former friend's father. "A little heads-up would've been nice."

"I hope you had a lovely day too, milaya." Her keys jangle as she puts them next to her bag on the laminate counter, eyeing the bowl of salted edamame sitting in front of me. Normally I'd have popcorn mixed with a healthy dose of M&Ms like I've been having every day since I got back, but after seeing Jasmine, I couldn't bring myself to do it. Unfortunately, soybeans were the next most appealing snack in the house. "And I didn't realize you needed to be told, given you were inseparable this summer. She didn't call you?"

I refuse to dignify that with a response and dig my teeth into another pod to scrape its insides.

"Ah. If it helps, it was a pretty last-minute decision, from what I gather. Declan didn't even enlist my help. I only found out today, when he told me to order flowers to his house to welcome her home from her first day."

I am slightly mollified by this, but still irritated overall. "Can I go to Shannon's for dinner?"

She sighs. "It's your first day of senior year, Larotchka. Possibly your last first day of school ever while living at home. Can you please humor your mother and tell her about it over frozen pizza?"

Now I feel like an asshole. It's not my mother's fault Jasmine is a jerk. "What kind of toppings do we have?"

"Only half a jar of olives, but they'll be delicious because they were added with love." She kisses the top of my head. "Go do your homework and I'll call you when it's ready."

I go to my room, but I don't start my homework. Instead, I head into my closet and stand on the lowest shelf to reach the scrapbook hiding on the highest one. Shannon would laugh her ass off if she knew I'd made something so sentimental. For that matter, so would Jasmine. But I'm relieved to have it, to have evidence this summer was real and not some wild delusion.

And there they are: ticket stubs from the movie theater in Kill Devil Hills, the Elizabethan Gardens, the Lost Colony show, and the ferry to Knotts Island. Photographs taken hugging lighthouses and pretending to fly in front of the Wright Brothers memorial. Papers from ice-cream cone wrappings, smooth shells from the beach, a joker from a well-used deck of cards, and even a cherry stem Jasmine tied into a knot with her tongue at a house party. There's no shortage of memories in these pages.

Truth is, I don't need snapshots or wrappers or stubs to remember this summer, despite some of it being hazy even while it was happening. Hell, even though I came back from that first party drunk as balls, I still remember every minute through at least the first three shots.

That was when I knew the summer might not suck.

THEN

I don't know what to wear to Jasmine's friend's party, not because I don't know how to dress, but because my summer nights were gonna consist of being a slug on the couch and binge-watching Netflix with my mom. I'd packed tons of bathing suits, shorts, and tanks, but for nighttime, all I have are a couple pairs of jeans and some cozy sleep pants in case I wanted to sit out near the water during chillier hours. Party clothes hadn't entered the equation.

Boring jeans and a polka dot tank top will have to do. Shannon would cringe if she saw me wearing flip-flops to a party, but Shannon is in Paris wearing heels and little scarves around her neck, so.

With nothing else to do, I'm ready embarrassingly on time, and, afraid to look overeager, I trap myself in my room, texting with Kiki and watching stupid YouTube videos. Finally, I hear movement outside, followed by "Tinkerbell, where are you?" hollered like a banshee.

I grab my bag and jolt off my bed to meet Jasmine, who looks a hundred times more stylish in a white tank top and pink capris, a row of bangles jangling on her arm. White is a color I avoid until we're at least two weeks into summer, but it pops enviably against Jasmine's naturally tan skin and dark, glossy hair.

I wait for a once-over, part of the pre-party ritual with Shannon, Gia, and Kiki, but all Jasmine says is, "Ready?"

I nod. It isn't until we're getting into her car that I ask, "Tinkerbell?"

"Tiny, blond, and could probably fit in my pocket. Plus, I still haven't perfected your mom's 'Larotchka.'"

I burst out laughing at her attempt at the wide-open A and the Russian roll of the R. For the most part, my mom's accent is only lightly traceable; she's been in the US since college. But when she says my nickname, it comes out in full force, and it's one of my favorite sounds in the world. It's weird to have someone so comfortably pick it up in a single day. Clearly, Jasmine has some powers of observation.

She grins and we hop in her Jeep, roll the windows all the way down, and turn the music all the way up. It's a band I've never heard before, all angry vocals and girlish whispers curling into screams, and it feels like writing my name in the sky with a stub of red lipstick. The salt air and the stilted houses are so wholly un–New York, not at all what I'd expected to experience this summer, and though none of it was my choice and all of it made me angry, tonight it's a kind of freedom.

I don't check Shannon's Instagram once. Or even Chase's.

The party house isn't as impressive as the Killarys', but it's decked out by someone who seriously knows how to host. We go right around to the beach, where flames from a fire pit lick the sky, dance music fills the air, and coolers of ice, soda, and beer dot the grass. There's a table full of little dishes of shrimp cocktail and crackers with speckled, cheesy spreads, and though every single chaise and beach chair in the entire Outer Banks seem to be in this one yard, every single one has a butt in it—in some cases, two butts attached to intertwined couples.

"Whose house is this?" I ask as we pick our way over to the drinks and I dutifully take a can of Diet Dr Pepper in adherence to my designated driver promise.

"Carter Thomas," she says, plucking the can from my hand and pressing a bottle of Corona into it instead. "I've thought about it and have come to the conclusion that making you DD on the night of your very first OBX party is too cruel, so *just this once*, I got it." She cracks open the can and takes a long, defiant drink, as if that ends the matter. And I suppose it does, because next thing I know I'm sipping from my beer and Jasmine is introducing me around.

It takes a while to find Carter, but until we do, I meet Owen, a red-faced white kid with a shock of carrot-colored hair and an easygoing, slightly gap-toothed smile; Keisha, Carter's cousin, whose dark skin shimmers with coconut-scented body glitter, a pleasant smell I pick up when she throws her arms around me in a warm hug that envelops me in her Minecraft T-shirt; Brea, who's maybe white or maybe Latina or maybe both and has long blond braids that whip in the wind and the kind of laugh that occasionally devolves into snorting, a.k.a. the best kind of laugh; and Derek, who's hot, East Asian, and would definitely be an interesting summer prospect if he weren't immediately joined by Jack, a dead ringer for Dax Shepard, who intertwines his fingers with Derek's and doesn't let go the entire night.

The funny thing about being in the Outer Banks only for the summer is that they're *all* only in the Outer Banks for the summer. The rest of the year they're scattered throughout the mid-Atlantic and the South, but they've all been coming here summer after summer since they were in swimmy diapers. It's clear this party is the traditional catch-up night, when Keisha tells everyone about her first year at Georgetown and Brea shares the latest about her hippie mother and Jack and Derek (Jerek?) show everyone pictures from their junior prom. On the one hand, I'm the obvious outsider. On the other hand, it's a perfect opportunity to slide right into the group—made distinctly easier when Owen brings us a platter of Jell-O shots.

"So, where are you from, new summer girl?" he asks as I help myself to a cup of cherry.

"New York. I live in a suburb outside the city."

He tosses back a cup of bright green. "And you're staying with Jas? How do you two know each other?"

An inevitable question, but ugh. It sounds so sad to say "We're staying in her house like indentured servants because my mom is her dad's secretary." I'm not ashamed of my mom's job or the fact that we don't have a lot of money, but I don't need people here treating me like I'm the hired help or whatever.

Luckily, Jasmine thinks much quicker on her feet than I do, answering while I down my Jell-O shot. "Our parents work together," she says, and I'm grateful for the non-lie. "Now, where the hell is Carter?"

"Someone call my name?" I look up and see a tall, muscular Black guy with close-cropped hair and dark, laughing eyes ambling over, the smile on his gorgeous face too perfect to be real. Turns out Carter's got waaay more than the house going for him. Yowza. "Hey, babe." He wraps an arm around Jasmine and kisses the top of her head in a way that's nowhere near as paternal as it sounds.

Of course she's got a guy here. So much for having someone to hang out with this summer. But that's probably a good thing. I was supposed to be making money to put toward college, and I had to give up my job to come here. I should be spending my time finding a new one.

I wonder if any of these kids have ever worked a day in their lives.

"Carter, this is Larissa," Jasmine introduces us. "Larissa, Carter. Now, how does a girl get a s'more around here?"

We make our way to the fire pit, and the girls surrounding it—who look no older than freshmen—scatter as we approach. Carter provides the supplies while Owen and Derek grab us more drinks. It takes a little more alcohol, but soon I'm relaxing and enjoying the sights and sounds of the party as much as everyone else. I dance with Owen, with Jack and Derek, with Keisha and Brea, with the group as a whole. By the time I notice Jasmine and Carter have disappeared, I'm pleasantly plastered and gossiping with these kids I've just met, so I immediately ask what their deal is.

"They just fool around," says Keisha, scooping sand onto her legs. "Nothing serious, but for the last few summers, like bunnies."

"Except for a couple of weeks two summers ago when Carter thought he'd met The One—remember that waitress at Sally's Seafood Shack?" Derek says. "What was her name again?"

"Marly!" the others shout, and then they fall apart laughing. Watching them be such a close-knit, comfortable group makes me miss the hell out of Shannon, Kiki, and Gia. But none of us are home for the summer. Shannon's in Paris, Gia's at cheer camp, and Kiki's in Japan with her grandparents. We're all living separate lives while everyone here is coming together.

I take a picture of the fire sparking into the sky, bottles dotting the sand around it, and text it to the three of them with a *Wish you were here.*

"So, Larissa, what's your story? Are you single?" Derek asks.

"Extremely," I say with a sigh that makes them all crack up.

"Well, that won't do," says Jack. "What's your pleasure? Boys? Girls? Both?" Keisha nails him in the side with an elbow, and he simultaneously coughs and laughs. "Sorry, *neither* is of course also an option. In this house, we respect aromantics and asexuals."

"*Thank* you," she says regally, resuming burying her legs.

"I'm not either of those," I say, quickly adding, "though we respect them in this house too. I'm a 'boys' person. Well, boy, in the singular; I don't think I'm cut out for more than one at a time." *In fact, there's only been one boy for a loooong time.* "But I'm not—I mean, there's kind of this guy."

Jack immediately drops his chin into his hands. "Do tell."

I can't help laughing. My friends at Stratford are so sick of my mooning over Chase, so I try not to do it too much, especially because it makes me feel pathetic. But here, I can spin it however I want, though I suspect these people would still think I'm fine if I reveal I've been crushing on a guy for years to no avail.

Pays to go somewhere for the summer where friends are slim pickings, I guess.

"He's a football player—the quarterback—and he's really talented, and he looks so damn good in the uniform," I begin, and I hear my voice take on a dreamy quality that makes me feel silly, but everyone is looking at me with rapt curiosity and I love this night so much. Another Jell-O shot finds its way into my hand and I suck it down without a second thought. "He's in my class and he's such a nice guy. Like, he's hot and popular and he could be such a dick, but he's always nice to everyone. I love that he's always nice to everyone." I'm babbling, like verbally foaming at the mouth, but I gave up any hope of catching his eye this summer when I came here, and it feels like I *deserve* this moment. "And he works so hard. I catch him in the gym *all* the time. Being good at what he does means so much to him."

Everyone nods like I'm not being incredibly boring, and I love them for it. Eventually, someone asks for pictures and I pass my phone around, feeling only a little creepy when Jasmine and Carter rejoin us and ask what we're up to.

I mumble a "nothing" into the summer air, but the others override me, making me love them a little less. I wait for the teasing to come, for this pair who've been off hooking up to mock my crush on a guy who's never so much as kissed my cheek, but it doesn't materialize. Instead, the conversation turns to old crushes. Everyone's in on it, from Brea laughing about her ancient unrequited love for her mom's yoga instructor to Keisha admitting she used to pull the "my boyfriend lives in Canada" move before she was out as aroace, and it's the most comfortable I've been in ages.

The comfort emboldens me to ask Jasmine about Carter when she's driving us back to her—our—house, and if she wants a window to confess deeper feelings, she's definitely got one. He seems like a really sweet guy, he's ridiculously hot, and he's cool as hell, so I'm expecting to pick up on some signals, even if she acts like it's nothing. Years of being friends with Kiki has taught me everything to look for, from dilated pupils to a flush in the cheeks to any number of tells in body language.

But all she says is, "It's nice to forget life for a while," and though I'm not sure it's her intended consequence, it shuts me up for the rest of the ride.

Chapter Four

NOW

The rest of the first week back goes the same—fun times with my girls, flirting with Chase, and complete and total avoidance of Jasmine while simultaneously obsessing. But it's Friday night, which means Chase's football game, followed by Jasmine's party, which means all this stuff hanging over my head is gonna have to go some kinda way.

Getting dressed for the night poses a problem. All my nicest new clothes are gorgeous, expensive things Jasmine tossed into my arms with a "Keep this; it'll look better on you." I'm sure as hell not wearing her castoffs to her party, which means avoiding several absolutely perfect outfits in favor of stuff I've worn a billion times. But at least I can play up the things that seem to be working for me, starting with this glorious tan that will be gone way too soon.

I do have a couple of new, cute tops just right for wearing to a game-party combo, so I dig through my drawers until I find the right one. It's white and cut high in front—my cleavage isn't exactly anything to write home about anyway—but dips all the way down in back. Jeans feel way too boring to wear to Jasmine's, especially with what's basically a T-shirt, so . . . aha! I knew I had these somewhere. When Shannon convinced me to buy leather shorts last year, I didn't think I'd ever have the guts to wear them. But last-year me only needed to wait a little longer for them to be perfect.

I officially look hot. No way Jasmine—er, *Chase*—isn't gonna notice.

My phone beeps as I'm finishing throwing a few things in my bag, and I know without looking that it's a *Where r u, bitch* text from Shannon. I always end up with one of those whether I'm late or not, but I throw on sandals and run out the door, yelling goodbye to my mom.

"I *told* you those shorts were a great purchase," Shannon says the instant I open the car door, and I let the relief of validation wash over me like a waterfall. "Now get your ass in here because my new mascara is a *godsend* and you are about to love me."

The mascara is indeed miraculous, and with a little brown eyeliner, a dab of highlighter, and a hint of lip gloss, I look understated and natural. To be honest, I would probably bang me. Shannon is a master at makeup application, and more importantly, she's generous with both her skills and her Sephora-size collection. I'm too busy preening for her "Looking good, Rissy" to irritate me.

"Chase is gonna die," Kiki confirms. Impending death is her greatest compliment, and I smile even wider.

The bleachers are full by the time the three of us roll in, but the nice thing about being that ideal combination of loved and feared is seats always seem to appear when you need them. We squish in a row toward the front of the center section, and my eyes immediately land on Chase, tall and lean in his navy-and-white uniform, with biceps so beautifully carved I want to lick them.

I've always loved watching Chase play—the way his muscles ripple when he pulls back his arm for a throw, the way his footwork looks like a manly dance . . . I know I'm biased, but he's genuinely good, good enough to play in college, which is his plan. (He also plans to major in sociology, though he'd be interested in sports medicine if he were better at science. Yes, I know a lot about Chase Harding's aspirations.)

Coach Montgomery calls a time-out and I use the opportunity to scan the crowd to see who else has shown up. I get a smile and wave from my lab partner, Jamie Nguyen, who's sitting with her—what do you call it when someone's neither a girlfriend nor boyfriend? Non-binary-friend?—Taylor, a cute junior with a mop of lavender curls, and I recognize a bunch of other random classmates. I *don't* see Jasmine.

That's no surprise. She's home prepping for her party. A party that could be ten people or a thousand, for all I know. She never actually confirmed I made the cut. But I'll be there, and my stomach is bubbling just thinking about it, wondering if her room is hiding memories similar to the ones I keep scrapbooked in mine. Is there a strip of pictures of us in her mirror? Or has everything faded away for her, the way it seemed to when we talked by her car?

I'm snapped out of my thoughts by the crowd erupting, and I jump to my feet along with everyone else, wondering if Chase ran in a touchdown.

At what point did I take my eyes off him, anyway?

"Harding is killing it tonight," a guy in front of me says to another, and my heart bursts with totally misplaced pride. For the rest of the half, I stay glued to every pass, every kick, every play. Harding *is* killing it tonight, and by the time the buzzer sounds at halftime, my heart is thumping in that old familiar way.

"I can smell the hormones dripping off you," Shannon says as she reaches into her purse and pulls out a pack of gum. She takes a piece and passes it down the line of us. "God, you still want him so bad."

There's never a point in denying anything to Shannon, so I don't. The gum is the perfect excuse for my mouth to be too busy to respond, and then Gia and the cheerleaders come out and we clap, whistle, and stomp as she shakes her pom-poms. I take a few pictures of her cheering, plus a couple of selfies with Kiki and Shannon, and I'm working on filtering and posting them when Shannon simultaneously coughs loudly and jabs me in the side with a bony elbow.

When I look up, there's the star himself, helmet off, hair soaked with sweat, his slightly crooked smile lighting up the entire field. "You came," he says, and it takes everything in my power not to look around to confirm he's talking to me.

I shrug, even though I can feel an unstoppable smile betraying me. "I heard Kosinski's aim really improved over the summer. Had to see for myself."

"And?"

God, there are so many people watching us. "I'd say you're all looking pretty good out there," I concede, and if possible, his smile dials up a few watts.

"Looking pretty good out here too," he says, and though my bare legs and back are hardly visible to him from that angle, I feel a little naked under his gaze.

I know this effect. He's had it on me for as long as I can remember. But since when do I have it on him?

He glances back at the field and it's clear he's gotta go back, but he turns to me again. "You going to the party tonight?"

The party. That's what it is to him. Not Jasmine's party, just *the* party. She does not factor into this equation. Not a bad thing for me to remember. "Planning on it."

"Good. I guess I'll see you there."

"Or you could drive her," says Shannon. "She could use a ride." The innuendo isn't lost on me, and I turn to glare at her. "What?" she says innocently. "Gia's gonna have all her cheer shit. I don't have room for all of that."

Shannon drives a fucking tank, but okay. I'm willing to bet Chase knows it too, but he says, "As long as you don't mind waiting for me to shower, I'm happy to take you."

I don't know whether to kiss Shannon or kill her, but Kiki declares that they'll keep me company until he's ready since they have to wait for Gia anyway, and before I know it I'm watching Chase jog back to the game with the knowledge that about a hundred people just watched that go down and the night has only just begun.

I'm gonna need more gum.

The Stratford Saints crush it, and Chase practically skips out of the locker room to pick me up from where Shannon, Kiki, and I are discussing celebrity bullshit. "I'm so flattered, being driven by tonight's MVP," I tell him with an exaggerated flutter of my lashes as we head out to his X-Terra. He laughs, but his joy and pride are palpable. It's one of the things I've always liked most about him—he wears whatever he's feeling on his sleeve.

It's also one of the things I've always hated. He's so clear about his emotions, I could never wonder if he might be secretly into me or hope he might be harboring a crush. But that clarity makes this moment, when I catch him shooting glances at the low back of my T-shirt, all the more delightful.

"As much as I love talking about myself and my win," he says once we're buckled in, "I wanna hear more about you. What'd you do this summer? Clearly you spent some time at the beach."

Talk about the last thing I wanna discuss. *Jasmine does not factor into this equation*, I remind myself, though we're literally going to her house. I take a deep breath. "Actually, I spent the entire thing at the beach. My mom and I went to the Outer Banks."

"Oh, where's that?"

I'd had the same reaction when my mom first mentioned it, although it seems impossible to imagine now.

While OBX is full of people from the mid-Atlantic down, up here, everyone with a summer house on the beach goes to the Hamptons. It's where I'd normally spend a week or two, lying out by the pool at the house Shannon's parents rent every summer. But though she extended the usual invitation so we could hang out before school started, I'd passed in favor of starting my job at the Book and Bean, where I *would've* spent the summer. It was beyond gracious of the owner, Beth, to give me another chance, including weekend shifts during the school year, and I wasn't gonna screw it up again—not with my car fund on the line.

Plus, it kept me busy, which was way better for distracting myself from Jasmine than lazing around a pool would've been.

"They're islands off the northern coast of North Carolina. You know Kitty Hawk?"

"First flight?"

"Yeah. That's there."

"Cool."

I'd thought so too. Jasmine had teased me mercilessly, but she took me there for a tour and a photography session in front of the monument until the heat wore us down. One of those photos was my phone wallpaper for a couple of weeks until I got sick of feeling like every time my phone lit up it was a challenge to call her, and I changed it to a picture of my mom and me instead.

"Oh, duh, I forgot to put in the address." Chase hands me his phone as he pulls out of the lot. "Can you check my texts? It should be the last one from Paulie."

I'm basking in the glow of being trusted with his text

messages, so it takes me a few beats to realize I already know the address. I've been to this house. Picking up and dropping off my mother as needed, even going inside once when she made me wait too long and I had to pee like a racehorse. I remember the bathroom being black marble, presided over by a light-up mirror. I remember very shiny wood floors. I remember thinking, "Jesus, this is a big house for one person."

But it isn't for one person anymore.

"It's thirty-seven Darlington," I tell him, typing it into his phone's GPS. His eyes are on the road; he can't tell I didn't check. And I don't want the temptation of his text messages, of knowing what girls' names I might see. If he and his cheerleader ex, Brielle, still talk, I definitely don't want to know. If there's a summer fling filling his inbox with heart emojis, that can stay in the vault.

We fill the space with easy and predictable conversation about the game, where we're applying for college, and what scouts he hopes are coming to check him out, but I don't expect any revelations, which is why I'm particularly surprised when he says, "Can I tell you something I haven't told anyone?"

"Of course," I say automatically, even though I know all I'll want to do with the secret is shout it from the rooftops to prove Chase Harding trusted me with special, classified information.

"Honestly, I'm hoping to stay local. Marist is pretty much my dream. It's D-I ball, and Poughkeepsie is only, like, an hour away. Plus, I look really good in red."

"I'll bet," I say, my heart fizzing at his confession.

"Is it Stratford you're so attached to, or your family, or what?"

"Both, I think," he says, and I pick up a tinge of a blush in the dark. "My brother goes to Arizona State because he wanted warmer weather and a fun party school, and he almost never makes it home. I don't wanna be that. I like doing holidays and stuff with my family, plus making my little sister be alone at home for everything would suck."

God, just when I thought my crush couldn't get any bigger. But then, Chase being an incredible big brother is one of the things that's always made my heart pitter-patter in the first place. His little sister, Kira, is a sophomore, and we were on the same Little League team as kids. He used to sit in the stands on the Sunday mornings he had free, holding massive homemade signs covered in terrible handwriting, and shout her name every time she came to bat.

At first, it made me sad I didn't have my own big brother.

Then it made me realize I wanted Chase Harding cheering for me.

And that's how it all began.

"This only child can confirm it would kinda suck," I say, although I've never known anything else, and I love my mom and our cozy holidays. But I'd be lying if I said I never wished there were more than the two of us at our small round table built for four. If I said I didn't occasionally wish we had a big ol' dining room to make festive and fill with stupid things like poinsettia placemats. If my heart hadn't twinged a bit on those summer nights when me, Jasmine, my mom, and Declan sat down to dinner together, feeling like a very weird but complete little family. Without even thinking, as we stop at a red light, I reach over and squeeze his hand. "You're a good brother."

He smiles softly. "Thanks."

Our hands stay locked until the light turns green.

The house is packed by the time we get there, with music blasting and people spilling out onto the lawn. We have to park two blocks away, which is perfect because it has Chase offering me his jacket to walk the distance.

I really, really want to say yes.

But Jasmine's first vision upon entering Stratford High was me flirting with Chase, and I find myself imagining how I'd feel if she walked into my house wearing someone else's jacket, and I can't do it. Not yet. Not until she and I talk.

"It's still pretty warm out, but thank you," I say, hoping my smile makes clear this is not a symbolic rejection. "But I'll take a raincheck for when it's chillier."

"Deal," he says, tossing his jacket back in the car, but he doesn't make a move to sling an arm around my shoulders or take my hand. I have to remind myself that a little space is what I implicitly asked for.

As the house—mansion?—comes into sight, I continue cycling through my Jasmine thoughts. What if she's every bit as cold tonight as she was outside school? What if she's already drunk? And the worst thought—what if she's with someone when we get inside?

Somehow I'm standing next to Chase fucking Harding, about to fulfill item number seven on my high school bucket list (rolling into a party on his arm), and I'm thinking about how badly I would want to throw up if I saw Jasmine Killary making out with someone on the other side of that door.

Literally everything is wrong with this picture.

What am I doing here?

I don't have a chance to rethink my plans, because the door swings open and a stream of Stratford kids comes pouring out. I recognize them as the tennis team, and a bunch of them say hi to us as they curl around the house and head into the yard. A quick peek past them shows it's probably too crowded inside to get to the French doors that exit to the deck with the hot tub, and oh God I remember this house so much better than I thought I did, which somehow makes everything feel worse.

The minute we walk in, Shannon, Kiki, and Gia descend on me, pulling me toward the kitchen while Chase accepts high fives and shoulder claps from adoring fans and teammates.

"So? How was the ride?" Kiki asks, waggling her eyebrows.

"Did you discuss his tight end?" Shannon's voice could not sound pervier.

Gia spares me—dirty humor isn't her thing—but her big Bambi eyes widen and I can tell she's waiting for a response.

I roll my eyes. "It was a car ride. We talked about normal things. We're friends. We talk about things."

"We're friends," Shannon says mockingly. "Oh, please. Fine, play it cool here, Bogdan, but when you're done with work tomorrow, we're going to Lily's and we're getting waffles and you are giving us a full—"

"Here you go, as promised!" A long, bronzed arm jangling with bangles reaches between us and holds out two long-necked bottles, which Shannon and Kiki pluck from familiar purple-tipped fingers. "And a cider for you." Jasmine hands a bottle to Gia with her other hand, and only when she has nothing left to offer does she realize I'm standing there with them. "Hey," she says with far less enthusiasm.

"Hey, yourself."

"Oh, you two have met!" Kiki says.

It's exactly the opening that can break open the truth. I could say, "We spent the summer together." I could say, "My mom works for her dad." But like with Chase's jacket, I don't want to make any moves until she and I talk—*really* talk—and I find out what the hell is going on.

"We're in English together" is all I offer, and I watch as Jasmine takes in my answer, takes in that I haven't told my friends about her. I try to convey with my eyes that it's a temporary response, that maybe it can change if she wants it to, but she just nods.

No upset, no surprise—just acceptance.

Suddenly, it's too much. It's all too much. The secrets and the summer hanging heavy between us and the meshing of my OBX life and my Stratford life, here in Jasmine fucking Killary's kitchen . . . it's too much.

"Can you show me where the bathroom is?" I ask Jasmine in a rush.

She starts to respond, and I motion as if I can't hear her. If she thinks she's getting out of having a real conversation, she's got another think coming. Thankfully, *that* she picks up on pretty quick, and soon she's leading me out of the kitchen and—as soon as no one's paying attention—up the stairs and to her bedroom.

It takes me a few seconds to realize that's what room we're in, because it looks so wildly unlike her, it's hard to imagine that this is where she sleeps. Even her vacation house had more personal character than this. There are no photos, no posters, no colorful scarves draped on anything, and she's gone from an entire case of books in her Outer Banks house to a single shelf here, most of which are for school. There isn't even any makeup strewn over her desk.

For the millionth time since I first spotted her in Stratford, I wonder if the Jasmine Killary I knew this summer was real.

"I see we're sticking with the secret route," she says, and I was so lost in observing everything that isn't there that I'm startled by the sound of her voice. I open my mouth to say that we don't have to, but she adds, "I think that's a good idea."

Even though I was expecting it, it feels like a shot to the heart. I don't answer right away, instead giving myself a little tour of her room. "Where's all your stuff?"

"In Asheville, mostly. My mom's selling the house and moving near family, so it didn't seem worth it to drag everything up here when I'd just be moving again next year."

Of course her mom would be selling their house, since it's the scene of one of my favorite memories of the entire summer. Burning those memories down seems to be the theme of the week. In another life, I would've asked how she feels about losing her child-hood home, and whether her mom's move is the reason she's here for the year, but we're in this alternate life now, so all I can do is make a stupid joke.

"I'm sure your dad would've sprung for a new *Crazy Rich Asians* poster. Hell, I can't believe you moved in without some sort of decorating clause in the contract."

Her only response is a little snort. Which means she's serious about not wanting to dig into our summer, to the many times we watched that movie together, to the day we found the poster at a dollar store and she declared she had to have it. She doesn't even want to take this op-portunity to talk about why, after ten years of a custody situation that's functioned like clockwork despite the frosty divorce behind it, things have suddenly changed.

She's serious about burying it all, which means I should be too.

"You really want to just pretend this summer never happened," I say, finally turning.

"Don't you?" she says, and I look up. Is that hurt in her eyes? It's impossible to tell when they're rimmed in kohl like that, glittering like liquid amber peeking from a cloud of smoke. And now that I'm meeting her gaze, I can't look away. She has this stupid fucking hold on me, and she knows it.

I've never been attracted to girls. I have lain awake

so many nights wondering, replaying nights in my mind of hanging out with Shannon, Kiki, Gia, Jamie, whoever, trying to find Signs. Objectively, they're all pretty, maybe even beautiful. But kissing them, touching them, being with them . . . it's never once crossed my mind. It still doesn't.

And I wasn't attracted to Jasmine like that either, at first. That's not what happened. I don't really *know* what happened. But I wasn't staring into her eyes like I am now, looking at her lips like I am now, remembering the feel of her skin on mine like I am now. It wasn't anything until it was, and then it wasn't, and now . . .

Now I am staring at The Spot on her neck and I cannot fucking stop.

I know exactly the sound she'll make if I touch my tongue to it. If I suck gently on it. If I suck not-so-gently on it. I can hear it in the vestiges of my brain and it's sending unwelcome waves of electricity right through my leather shorts.

I know the sound she'll make and I know what it does to me and she knows what it does to me and what to do next. Like a faraway dream I see exactly how this night can progress if we just shut her goddamn door and forget that there's an outside world, that there's a party downstairs and a boy at that party who's supposed to be the only one who makes me feel like this.

"We should go downstairs," she says, her voice hoarse. "People will be wondering where we are."

People. Shannon. Gia. Kiki the Detective.

Chase.

"Yeah," I say. I sound just as hoarse. And I don't

really want to go downstairs. But staying here isn't an option. I wait for her to leave, but she doesn't.

So I do.

"There you are!" Chase finds me as soon as I make it downstairs, and despite my libido having gone into overdrive with Jasmine, the smile that lights up his face makes my stomach do a very familiar flip. God, I am a terrible person. A terrible, horny person. "I thought I lost you. Everything OK?"

I can feel Jasmine's eyes on us, watching as he rests a hand comfortably on my back as if there's always been a space for him. In a way, I guess there has. She wasn't there for my full-on gushing about him to our OBX friends, but she knows exactly who he is.

Suddenly, my skin feels prickly and itchy and I need to get out of her line of vision. "I'm fine," I assure him. "Or I will be once I get your ass on the dance floor."

He laughs. "Lead the way, madam."

When I'm sure she can no longer see us, I relax, moving my body along with his to the music. His hands are firm and warm on my hips, and I feel other people watching, sizing up the situation. But I'll take a thousand eyes of Stratford onlookers over two of Jasmine's intense, inquisitive ones any day.

"Shamir special?" Two deeply tanned hands extend red Solo cups our way, and I see they're attached to Shamir Ben-Dror, who fancies himself an amateur bartender but only makes anything remotely potable about forty percent of the time. I think about accepting one anyway, but things already feel so loaded. I'm afraid I'll do something even more stupid than I almost did upstairs if I get a drink into my system.

"I'll pass, but thanks." I look at Chase. "Feel free to help yourself. I'm happy to be designated driver if you trust me with your keys. You should be celebrating."

He grins, and it's too freaking adorable. "You are a very cool girl, Larissa Bogdan. I'll take one of those, Shamir, my man."

"Bottoms up!" says Shamir, and he hands Chase a cup. They clink their drinks, and I watch Chase down his and look like he's gonna puke. While I pray vomit isn't in my future, it'd probably be worth it to hear "You are a very cool girl, Larissa Bogdan" over and over again in my dreams.

Never mind it's Jasmine who taught me how much it can mean to offer to be DD.

I am definitely not thinking about that.

I am not thinking about her at all.

Chapter Five

I get home fifteen minutes after my midnight curfew, but the deal is as long as I text before twelve to say I'm fine and running late, I'm OK. I'd texted at a quarter to, when it was obvious that driving a plastered Chase home in his car with Shannon following in hers to bring me home afterward wasn't going to be without time delays, so I'm in the clear. But when I let myself inside and find my mom up and waiting on the living room couch, I worry that I've misstepped.

I'm even more concerned when she asks, "How was Jasmine's party?" as soon as I close the door behind me.

"Good," I say cautiously, positive I never told her exactly what I was doing tonight. "How'd you know it was Jasmine's party?"

My mom has a very knowing smile that I absolutely hate, and there it is. "You think she planned that whole thing on her own in a single week? Please."

"Ugh." I drop onto the other end of the couch and

pry off my strappy sandals. "You being involved in my social life to that extent is officially weird."

"But it was a good party, wasn't it?"

"It was," I grudgingly admit. I should've guessed my mom had something to do with it when I spotted the pickle-flavored potato chips. My mom is always trying to make those happen. She's convinced if people just *tried* them, they'd fall in love. So far, she's converted exactly no one. I'm pretty sure that bowl was still seventy-five percent full when I left, and I'd eaten most of it. What can I say? I've gotten used to the taste. My mom loves pickled *everything* and her Russian genes run strong. "But it would've been better at Hunter Ferris's house."

"Because I wouldn't have had anything to do with it?"

"Because Jasmine has been kind of a bitch ever since she got to Stratford." Somehow, without any drinks in me, the words I've been dying to speak come loose. "She's trying to pretend we were never friends—don't ask me why." *No, really, don't ask me.* "She's barely acknowledged we've met before this."

Okay, that might not be the most even-handed presentation, but whatever. My mom, my side of the story.

"Oh, milaya, that doesn't sound right." Mama reaches out and strokes my bobbed hair, and suddenly I'm aware of how much shorter it is than the shoulder-blade-sweeping style I used to wear. "You two were so close. She's probably trying not to be overly dependent on you for a social life. Make her own way and all that."

"Why? She'd be well within her rights to jump into

my social circle," I say, even though I'm relieved she hasn't. "Lord knows that's exactly what I did with hers."

"Yeah, but you know Jasmine. She's very . . . independent. She wants to do things herself."

My eyebrows shoot up. "And I'm not independent? Are you saying I'm a leech?"

"Bozhe moi." She sighs deeply, like she always does when she thinks I'm pushing teenagedom to the max. "Lara, I did not call you a leech. But you do have a tendency to rely on other people rather than forging your own path, and that's not what Jasmine's like."

"You know I'm even *more* offended now, right?" I say, pulling away from her hand.

She closes her eyes. "Of course you are. I think that's my cue to go to bed. Spokoynoy nochi, milaya. We'll talk tomorrow when it's not so late." She kisses the top of my head and pads off to her bedroom.

While my mom is following up her ill-fated motherly talk with a good night's sleep, I'm wide awake in my room, pacing and looking through all my pictures, old postcards, and other souvenirs. My mom doesn't know what she's talking about; my whole world is evidence I'm a freaking social butterfly.

I mean, yes, okay, Shannon is definitely the social director of our group, but who cares? That's one of the reasons I love Shannon—she's such a caretaker in her own weird way, and she knows the rest of us can't plan shit. It doesn't bother Kiki or Gia how often she takes charge. And yeah, Shan usually chooses where we're going, but in fairness, she's always the one driving.

But also, it's not like they're my only friends. I'm friends with Jamie, and kind of with Taylor. And with Deanna, who sits next to me in Spanish—we talk during class all the time. And Chase! Chase and I are *certainly* friendly these days.

So there, Mother.

And it's not just school. I had a great summer with Keisha, Derek, Owen, Brea, Jack, Carter, and She Who Must Not Be Named. She wasn't even *present* when I marathoned the Star Wars movies with Keisha, or for either of the two times I joined Brea and Derek at hot yoga.

I'm feeling smug and self-satisfied for all of two seconds when the doubt starts creeping in.

Kiki has a podcast, *Kiki on the Case,* and has all these internet friends from this online forum dedicated to unsolved mysteries, plus the Asian American Students' Association, whose meetings she attends whenever she needs a break from what she lovingly (I think) calls our Unbearable Whiteness of Being.

Gia has a boyfriend she's practically married to and the very same cheerleading squad I quit.

Shannon does random sophisticated shit, like museum outings and French Club, and has a new boy on her arm every five minutes. She's the kind of person who not only has a five-year plan but will definitely execute every single step perfectly, while still managing to be the absolute most fun person in the world to party with *and* the one who'll have the perfect hangover cure in the morning.

What the hell do I have besides a few secret files on my

computer all called some variation of TerribleWriting.doc? Would the four of us have stayed friends for as long as we have if Shannon and her plans hadn't kept us together?

As for my summer friends, I haven't exactly done a stellar job of keeping in touch: a "like" of Brea's post about some yoga achievement here, a sad face emoji on a picture depicting Derek and Jack parting for the school year there. . . . At most there were a few texts between me and Keisha, casual reminders that a show we liked had its season premiere coming up. I'd had a great time with them all, but the closer Jasmine and I got, the further the others had faded into the background. I still scrolled through their pictures to see Keisha with the marching band friends she'd talked about all summer, Owen's surfing action shots, and Carter's Outfit of the Day posts, but without Jasmine to share them with, it felt like another life.

Without Jasmine, I don't have OBX friends.

Without Shannon, would I have Stratford friends?

If I somehow got Jasmine back—if I even *wanted* her back—what would it mean losing when everyone else found out the truth?

I press a pillow over my mouth and scream in frustration. Damn my mother for starting me down this train of thought.

When I finally tuck myself into bed, I make myself think happy thoughts of Chase as I fall asleep, but I end up dreaming of an empty beach.

I wake feeling like crap the next morning, but while dear old Dad has agreed to subsidize my college tuition as long as I go to a state school, I'm on my own for the Larissa Bogdan Automobile Fund, so off to work I go.

The bookstore-slash-café is surprisingly busy on weekend mornings, which I guess is why Beth Rinker, a.k.a. the owner of the Book and Bean, was kind enough to take me in when I came crawling back. It officially opens at 9:00 a.m. on Saturdays, but I get there at 8:00 a.m. to prep the machines and display cases and get brewing behind the café counter.

That hour is unexpectedly pleasant, with no noise but the hum of the coffee makers and the smooth thwack of Beth shifting books. It gets even better when I get to make myself a steaming hazelnut-scented mug of coffee and top it off with a dollop of whipped cream. For Beth, I make it black—"like my soul," she instructed me when I first started. One of many reasons I love Beth.

There's a small line of customers by a quarter after nine, most of whom I recognize from the past few weeks: Alice, the mom who brings her twin toddlers, and refers to her regular order of an enormous black coffee with two shots of espresso as her "life essence"; Dave, the guy who buys exactly one small coffee and sits hunched over his laptop nursing it for half my shift, writing what I'm pretty sure (and I hope) is a spy novel, judging by the websites I've seen open on his screen for research; a goth girl, who mumbled her name the first time and never bothered repeating it, but always gets something sugary and frothy; and some days (though not often, because my mom rarely spends money on anything frivolous), there's my mom and her "surprise me" order, though we both know only the most bitter of drinks will do.

The guy at the front of the line now, despite looking familiar, is someone I'm pretty sure I've never served coffee to. I've got a pretty good memory for regular orders, but I'm drawing a blank on him.

"How can I help you?"

He holds up a book, and I recognize the illustrated cover immediately. "You recommended this book for my daughter the last time I was here, and I wanted to say thank you. She absolutely loved it and begged me to come back for the rest of the series."

The image makes me smile, though it's bittersweet. Jasmine's the one who originally recommended the Candy Buttons graphic novel series to me. When I happened to catch this guy asking Beth for a recommendation for his daughter who's not a big reader, I had to swoop in and suggest graphic novels might do the trick. And, of course, I had to make some suggestions when he asked. *Candy Buttons* was a natural choice, since I'd already suggested Beth buy it for the tiny section that was almost entirely (the excellent but far more obvious) Raina Telgemeier and *Lumberjanes*. I mentioned a few more of Jasmine's favorites as well, which Beth ordered for him on the spot. I couldn't believe either of them had trusted me so readily, but here was proof I knew what I was talking about.

Or at least Jasmine did.

"We definitely have the second book here," I assure him, "and I'm sure Beth will be happy to special order the third. It comes out next week."

"I'll go ask her right now, thank you."

I expect him to walk away, but he doesn't, and I realize he might actually want some coffee. "Did you want a drink too?"

"No, I just . . . really wanted to thank you. I'm never the hero with gifts for her. I always manage to fu—uh, screw it up. This is the first time I've ever nailed it, and it's a big deal. So . . . yeah. Thank you."

It's a good thing I'm definitely not tearing up because the room is already somehow getting blurry. "You are very, very welcome," I say, and God, I hate that I can't tell Jasmine. Her secret mushball heart would melt. "I have plenty more recommendations when you run out."

"You're wasting your time behind this counter," he says. "You should be in sales."

Well, there's no great way to admit I lost that position when my mom made me bail, and now I have to watch this random college kid named Greg suck at it. He literally goes entire days without recommending a single author who isn't an old white guy. I'd tell Beth how much he sucks, but I'm pretty sure she knows, and it makes me feel bad. She must've been really desperate to have hired him. "Feel free to tell Beth I deserve a raise," I say instead. He laughs as he leaves, but somehow, I think he'll do it.

The rest of the morning continues like normal, but that interaction stays with me for a while, including during my break, when I treat myself to a white hot mocha. (I'm allowed one fancy drink every half a shift, I swear.) I'd been completely stunned by Jasmine's reading choices over the summer, assuming she was one of those chic ice princesses who always seemed to be reading *Anna Karenina,* but the way she told it, her mom got her started with *Persepolis* by Marjane Satrapi and *Maus* by Art Spiegelman, and a love of reading words mixed with visuals fell into place.

She lent me book after book, though I only got through maybe a quarter of what she did. I had no idea speed-reading was a real thing until I watched her devour four books in a single day. We spent a lot of time at the Kill Devil Hills Library, enjoying the air conditioning and browsing the artful displays. Jasmine was horrified to learn I'd given up a job at a bookstore to come to OBX. Apparently, she'd dreamed of being a librarian as a kid, something she confided she'd never told anyone else. Web design and photography were more her thing now, but she said even if she kept up with them in college, in reality, she was probably gonna go to business school and do something boring.

I really, really hoped she wouldn't.

"Hey, Larissa." I look up to see Beth standing in front of the counter, a pile of flyers in her hands. "Can you hang these up around the store, and take a few to hang up around town?"

"Sure." I take a bunch from her and skim the paper. "Holy crap, you're getting Clementine Walker to the store?"

"You've read her stuff?"

"Every single book." I look at the date. It's a Sunday, two days after Homecoming, but no matter how exhausted I am, I will absolutely be here working.

Jasmine's bookish thing is graphic novels; mine are smutty romances with a heavy dose of humor, and Clementine Walker is the best of the best. She's the author who first made me want to try my hand at writing my own. Jasmine read a few of her books in exchange for my reading *her* favorites, and let's just say they went over *very* well.

Goddammit, it would be really fun to bring her to this.

And yet, the thought of her doesn't conjure her presence. Instead, it conjures Chase Harding, who comes ambling over to the counter, flashing Beth a smile that could definitely lighten the darkest of souls. "Hey," I say, and I can't help smiling too, even though I have no idea what he's doing here. In the past I would've frozen up at a surprise Chase sighting, but now I feel like I could chat with him over hot mocha lattes for an hour. "Beth and I were just talking about my favorite romance author coming to town." I hold up a flyer. "Please tell me you're a closet fan."

"Oh, nothing closeted about my fandom for . . ." He squints at the flyer. "Clementine? Isn't that a fruit?"

"A fruit *and* a killer name for a killer author." I take a flyer and pin it on the bulletin board, glad I wore my good-butt jeans to work today. I feel his eyes on my backside like laser beams. "So, what's up? You here for a drink? I make a mean chai latte."

"Sure, I'll take one of those," he says, leaning against the counter and pulling out his wallet. The bell over the front door tinkles, and Beth scurries off to welcome the new customer, since we both know Greg won't. "I also wanted to thank you for driving me home last night, and make sure you got back okay."

I make change from his ten and note with satisfaction that he leaves a tip in the jar. "Oh, I was actually murdered last night, but doesn't my ghost look fantastic?"

He grins. "It sure does. Which brings me to the other reason I'm here—to see if you're free tonight. I thought it might be nice to hang out without two hundred of our closest friends."

For a moment, as I pour from the pitcher of chai I prepared that morning into a hot cup, all I can think is that I need a Q-tip to clean out my ears. Because I could swear Chase Harding just strolled into my place of employment and asked me on a date. Like it was no big deal. Like he would enjoy hanging out and possibly buying me a burger or holding hands throughout a movie.

It's a very weird thing when you have imagined something happening for God knows how many years and then it . . . does.

A ridiculous part of me wants him to take it back, because as soon as it's out there, I miss waiting for it, dreaming of it. And it doesn't feel like I thought it would either. It feels like . . . a question. A question I could easily say yes or no to. A question that isn't the be-all and end-all of everything.

And then I realize the answer actually *is* no, and there's a little twinge in my gut.

"I'm babysitting tonight," I say with a frown as I carefully add hot, frothy milk to his drink. I'm tempted to cancel on the Sullivans and their triplets, but I don't want to give up a really, really well-paying job, nor do I want to wreck their monthly date night. "Maybe tomorrow? I work the same shift here as today, but I'm free after that." Well, I have a paper due for European history I've barely started, and I promised my mom I'd work on my college apps this weekend and also do the laundry at some point, but besides that.

It's *Chase Harding.*

My mom will understand.

"I'm playing basketball with the guys in the afternoon. After, we're hitting up Benny's. You're welcome to come." It's obvious from his voice he realizes it's a lousy offer, joining a bunch of guys from the team at their favorite diner for pastrami sandwiches, guaranteeing unkissable breath. But the truth is, I like the guys on the team, and I like Benny's fried chicken sandwiches. Still, I appreciate his follow-up of "I promise you ice cream afterward."

"Well, how can I say no to an offer like that?" I ask as I add a dusting of cinnamon to his drink and push it forward.

"You definitely can't," he says, and there's that grin. God, he's cute. And this is so easy. How is this so easy?

Don't you dare overthink this, Larissa.

"Well then—text me when you're done with your game? *After* you've showered, that is," I add with an exaggerated wrinkle of my nose, even though all I smell is the spicy drink sitting between us on the counter.

He laughs. "Deal. But I don't think I have your number."

That was the point.

He hands over his phone. "Put it in?"

So many dreams suddenly coming true in one place. God, I can't wait to tell Shannon. She's going to want to do a full-on makeover night. Except I'm pretty damn happy with how I already look, and it seems Chase is too.

Whatever, I'll deal with that when the time comes. For now, I take Chase's phone, type in my number, and hand it back. "There. Now text me so I have yours."

Yes, I could've done it myself. But that is not how dream fulfillment works.

He types something into his phone, and a moment later, mine buzzes. A winking emoji. Followed by an ice cream emoji. They look kind of pervy together, but I feel pretty okay with that.

A loud cough sounds from behind Chase's lanky form, and I realize a line has formed behind him. "I'll be right with you, sir," I say to the next customer, then glance back to Chase. "Did you want anything else this morning?"

"Nothing I can't wait for a little longer." And he winks. And I die.

He takes his drink and walks away, and I stare at his ass the entire time.

My throat is suddenly impossibly dry. "Next!"

Despite my wish-fulfillment morning, I'm back to thinking about how frustrating the situation is with Jasmine as I put the Sullivan triplets to bed that night. For some reason, I expected her to come walking through the door to the Book and Bean, order a double shot of espresso, and browse the shelves. One of the hardest parts of leaving Asheville for Jasmine must've been leaving behind her favorite bookstore, and it's not like every city in Westchester has one. The Book and Bean should've been at the top of her list of places to explore.

She must know I work there.

And these are the lengths she's going to in order to avoid me.

Not that I wanted her to come in. I mean, yeah, if it were like old times and we could chat about *Goldie Vance* and play "Judge a Book by Its Cover" (wherein we made up absolutely ridiculous stories about what books were about based on their packaging) and I could squee to her about Clementine Walker. If that were on the table, if we could just freaking be *friends*—

It hits me like the pudding cup little Ashlyn threw at me after dinner. What if the problem is she thinks I want more than that? What if she thinks I'm after the, uh, not-exactly-friendly stuff we did, and this is her way of letting me down? I mean, yeah, that's pretty arrogant and ridiculous to assume without talking to me, but Jasmine doesn't exactly win awards for her communication skills, and in fairness, neither do I.

Tomorrow, I'm going on a date with Chase and word is undoubtedly gonna spread about it. Maybe that's all we need. Maybe once she knows my heart and libido lie elsewhere, she'll chill out and we can go back to being friends, minus the benefits.

"Why are you smiling?"

Shit, my brain went off the rails while I was still standing in the triplets' room, and Chadwick has caught me looking like a goof. Their night-light must've been illuminating my face in creeptastic fashion. "Go to sleep," I say, slipping out the door, but I'm still smiling as I shut it behind me.

Chapter Six

Sunday's shift is much like Saturday's, minus the surprise drop-in by Chase and the early-morning heartwarming moment, but it feels like it takes three years longer. The minutes tick by slowly as I wait until I can go home and get ready for my date. Is it a date? I'm not sure it counts if it also includes half the football team. (Though some might say that makes it a really, *really* good date.) But he'd been going for a date when he initially invited me out—of that I'm at least eighty percent sure—so I'll take this in the spirit it's probably intended.

The thing is, I've had the perfect dress picked out for my first date with Chase for years, but as I stand in front of my closet, holding it in hand, it suddenly feels like . . . too much. I'd always imagined when we finally went out, it would be to a romantic dinner at one of my favorite restaurants—maybe one of those pretty spots right on the Long Island Sound. No one dreams of their first date being a casual evening with the guys at a diner.

How does one dress for looking sexy with pastrami breath?

My fingers are itching to ask Shannon for advice, which is what I'd normally do. We know each other's closets as well as our own. Even if she gives good advice, she'll be thinking this is a bullshit date, and I'm not in the mood for it. Gia would be stressful in the complete opposite way; I don't want to listen to what a huge deal this is for an hour either. And unfortunately, Kiki's useless for fashion advice. Her idea of mixing up her black-and-gray wardrobe is to add pinstripes.

Jasmine would've been the perfect call. Shopping with her was one of my favorite things to do because she's honest to a fault, but when you find something that looks good—and she would make me try on some craaaazy shit because she was certain it'd look fantastic on me, and was often right—she makes you feel like no one has ever looked as good in anything as you look right then in that rhinestone-studded leather bodice.

There *is* a great dress I'd purchased with her at the outlet mall in Nags Head, and it's still summery enough outside to wear it, though the bright red gingham feels a little country against the backdrop of Stratford. Well, whatever—I spent the money and I know it looks cute on me. I shuck off the black yoga pants and matching T-shirt I've worn under my purple apron for the past six hours and jump into the shower.

Forty-five minutes later, I'm clean, cute, and my mom is driving me to Benny's, Demi Lovato's "Confident" bursting from the car's speakers. (I embark on approximately nothing without blasting this song first.

Thankfully, my mom understands.) But my enthusiasm comes to an abrupt halt when I see waaay more cars in the parking lot than I expected, including a familiar 4Runner.

So much for Shannon not having the info to mock this non-date.

There's a little less bounce in my espadrilled step when I let myself into the diner, even though Shannon whoops when I walk in and loudly proclaims what a cute cowgirl I make.

Thankfully, I'm saved from having to respond by Chase getting up like the gentleman he is and giving me one of those epic smiles. "You came!" he says, as if it were ever a question.

"How could I pass up a fried chicken sandwich with extra slaw?" Out of the corner of my eye, I see Shannon registering that Chase's invite is why I'm here. I also see her flirting with Lucas Miller, which I guess explains why *she* is.

I am not looking forward to the hour of "How could you not tell me?" that will go down the instant I get home.

And speaking of conversations I'm not looking forward to, everyone jumps right back into the one they were having before I arrived, which was about Friday's party and its mysterious hostess. "So, nobody knows if she has a boyfriend?" Keith Radcliffe asks.

The question sits in my stomach, heavy as a stone. It doesn't help when Shannon pipes up, "Sure didn't seem like it when she was dancing up on Linus Friday night."

Ugh, *Linus*? Of all people? God, he's the kind of guy

who thinks negging is a legitimate social interaction. How do you go from me, or even Carter, to *that*?

"Linus is a douche," says Keith, and I can't argue with him there. "She can do way better. She's got a bangin' body."

Okay, now Keith is a douche. Discussing a girl's body in public is gross, and anyway, he's barely even seen it. Like, yeah, OK, sure, you know what she looks like because you've seen her in a short skirt. Maybe don't think you know her "bangin' body" before you've ever come face-to-face with her hip bones because let me tell you, you don't know jack shit.

"Hey, you OK?" Chase murmurs in my ear.

I blink out of my ragey hornball thoughts. "Yeah, of course. Why?"

"Because you've massacred my fries."

I look down and see a ketchup-bloody pile of potato stumps scattered around a red basket coffin. "Whoops." My cheeks fill with heat. "Sorry about that. Guess I'm hungrier than I thought. Where's our waitress?"

Chase gives me a funny look. "I already ordered for you—fried chicken sandwich with extra slaw, right? And I was planning to share my fries, but maybe I should order more of those."

"I'll get them," I say sheepishly, climbing out of the booth. I need some air, even if it's heavily scented with cooking oil.

I don't know what's wrong with me. This is it. This is everything. I'm on a date-ish thing with Chase and my best friend is here (for better and for worse) and he *ordered* for me and everyone knows it and somehow

Jasmine is managing to ruin it without even being present.

In another life, having her around could make sense. She could date Keith and I could date Chase and we could double, or even add Shannon and Lucas and triple. It'd be perfect.

Except we're in this life, and that sounds like my personal hell.

I order fries and they tell me they'll bring them to the table, so I have no choice but to go back. I hope they'll be done talking about Jasmine by the time I arrive, but no such luck. Worse, I get there as Shannon's assuring everyone that she and Jasmine are friends and she'll get the dirt on if she's seeing someone.

The idea of Shannon and Jasmine being friends is an immediate appetite killer.

My relationship with Shannon is complicated, but she's still my best friend. She'd drag someone over broken glass for hurting me, and yes, I do say that from experience. She may like to keep her friends in line, but she would also do anything for us, and I don't exactly have a lot of people like that in my life. (Shout-out to my dad, wherever he is these days!)

So, yeah—the only thing I might hate more than the idea of losing Shannon to Jasmine is the idea of losing Jasmine to Shannon.

And if the two of them get close and start sharing secrets about me, I might lose them both.

I am so not letting that happen.

"When did you guys become so tight?" I ask as casually as I can manage while I squeeze back in next to Chase, sitting a little closer to him than before. "I didn't realize you'd hung out. You don't think she's a little weird?"

I honestly don't even know what about her I could play off as weird, but desperate times, etc., etc.

"We talked for a while at the party," Shannon says, "and I didn't get a weird vibe. She's pretty cool. She speaks French even better than I do and she's been, like, everywhere. All the jewelry she was wearing came from a trip to Morocco."

My brain immediately corrects this piece of information. She was also wearing the emerald ring her grandparents gave her for her sixteenth birthday, bought for her in Paris. Plus, she always wears her hamsah-and-Jewish-star necklace underneath her clothing, and that was a bat mitzvah gift from her mom. They're silly facts, but knowing them reminds me that it'll be a while before Shannon can surpass everything I know about Jasmine. Because, apparently, I've created a competition in my head, and I'm not going down without a fight.

"Why don't I invite her here?" Shannon continues, pulling out her phone. "Keith can lay on the charm right now."

The only part of me that doesn't want him to call her bluff is the part that wants to know if Shannon really has Jasmine's phone number. Thankfully, Keith is a total coward and says his romantic moves are not meant for a greater audience. While everyone's teasing him, the food arrives, and thankfully, the conversation changes to things like scouts, college applications, and Homecoming. I swear Chase squeezes my thigh when the latter comes up.

Homecoming on Chase Harding's arm? I'm not sure I've allowed myself to dream that high. (That's a lie—I have quite literally had this dream many, many times, and I always wake up in a terrible mood when I realize it's just the work of my horny brain. It is item number two on my high school bucket list, right behind "prom on Chase Harding's arm.") But now he's here, ordering me a fried chicken sandwich with extra slaw and squeezing my thigh and making no secret of the fact that he's interested. It's all so fast I'm starting to get paranoid Shannon's behind it, like she's paid him to make my senior year special or something. Which is ridiculous, because honestly, I don't really lack for confidence, but how else do I explain such a huge change?

"You still up for ice cream after this?" His low voice tickles my ear and beyond, and suddenly, I wouldn't care if my own mother was paying him for this.

"Absolutely," I say, and this time when his hand squeezes my thigh, it stays put.

As expected, I get an eyebrow waggle and a mouthed "Call me" from Shannon when Chase and I take off after dinner. It's surreal that I'm already getting to know his car, like the way the AC vents need to be jiggled and how classic rock always fills the air within seconds of him starting the car. That he'll tap the beat on the steering wheel any time a Rolling Stones song comes on, and he won't *do* air guitar when it's Black Sabbath, but his fingers will twitch like he wants to and is controlling himself in front of me.

So many things to learn about this boy I've been observing for as long as I can remember.

I know he's gonna get vanilla with rainbow sprinkles because I've seen him here with his friends and that's what he got both times. He doesn't disappoint. I get the same because I spent the whole ride thinking about how I knew he was gonna get it and by the end of the five-minute ride to the Ice Palace, I couldn't get the craving out of my head.

"You know, everyone else teases me about how boring I am," he says as we sit down on one of the benches outside. "You didn't have to get the same thing to make me feel better."

"As it happens, I think vanilla is extremely underrated," I tell him as I lick a stray drop off my finger, knowing he's watching me do it. I actually *do* think vanilla is underrated, but yeah, under normal circumstances I probably would've gotten cookie dough or one of those flavors with seventeen kinds of candy bar in it. "And so is a little colorful brightness on dessert."

"*Thank* you," he says, a huge smile breaking out onto his face. "How do you not get in a good mood eating something covered in bright colors? My little sister taught me that."

God, I wish he hadn't mentioned Kira. My crush on him grows three sizes whenever he does. #onlychild problems.

And then my stomach twinges again because "hashtag onlychildproblems" was something Jasmine and I used to say all the time.

I'd been so upset at the thought of Shannon calling

her when we were at Benny's, but why didn't *I* just do it? My mom's right, at least in part—I did depend on Jasmine for friends in the Outer Banks. Shouldn't I be making it up to her for introducing me to Keisha, Derek, and the rest by inviting her out with *my* friends?

Even if I'm worried Shannon might steal her.

Or Keith might.

Or both.

What does it matter anyway, if I have Chase?

That's the million-dollar question, I guess.

But also, I don't quite have Chase yet. And if I want to, I should probably talk instead of staring out into space, letting the ice cream melt over my hands. After a while, there's no way to make cleaning that up look sexy.

I take another lick of the cone and look at this boy who has starred in my dreams. He's looking back at me, with those beautiful eyes the color of the night sky, and I somehow feel warm and shivery at the same time.

"It's clear I'm gonna kiss you now, right?" he asks, and I nod.

I had always imagined sparks the first time I kissed Chase Harding, but it's a sweet, cold kiss, thanks to the ice cream, and sprinkles feel better than sparks, anyway. We can't exactly get handsy while holding our cones, but it's definitely more than a peck, and I'm hyperaware of his scruff against my skin.

It's hard to forget that the last person you spent weeks kissing was a smooth-skinned girl when you feel that scruff again.

But it sure doesn't mean they can't both feel good.

We finish our ice cream and head back to his car, where some more kissing happens before we drive home to Rush and The Who. There's more kissing in my driveway. We finally jump apart when my cell phone rings, revealing Shannon's face on the screen. But whatever, I'm in a good mood and I *want* to talk about my night, so hopefully she's up for being excited rather than a buzzkill. One never knows how generous she's feeling.

Chase laughs quietly as I silence my phone and says, "Guess I should let you go, but maybe next Friday night, after the game, we can do this 'just the two of us' thing again?"

"Weren't the guys talking about going to Lucas's after the game?"

"The guys were." He tucks a blond curl behind my ear. "I wasn't."

Oof, that was good. I debate just how smutty it would be to haul him into the back seat of his car and decide it might be a bit much. But that won't stop me from being a little shameless. "Sounds good. Maybe pick a terrible movie we can not-watch."

"God, I like you," he murmurs, and though I can't respond through him kissing me, "I like you too" shimmers through my entire body.

It only makes sense that Jasmine Killary would be the first person I see at school Monday morning. She's standing near my locker, and I'd almost think she was waiting for me, if she weren't so consistently clear that waiting for me isn't something she'll ever be doing again.

"I hear you and Chase Harding are officially a thing."

I freeze in my tracks. There's only one person who'd have told Jasmine, only one person who sat with me on the phone for an hour last night until she'd squeezed out every bit of information. "Apparently, so are you and Shannon."

"I knew he was gonna be all over you as soon as he saw you," she says, sidestepping my response. "I told you that hair would be great on you."

The fact that she's taking any credit for Chase and me getting together when she's the one preventing me from fully enjoying it pisses me off, and of course she managed to poke at the very thing I've been most worried about. "I don't think a cut 'n' color can be credited for an entire relationship, Jasmine." *I hope not, anyway.*

"No, I suppose not," she muses. "But you have this whole . . . aura of confidence that's a way more magnified version of when I met you. Has he found your piercing yet?"

The piercing. We were so bored one day that a game of Truth or Dare? went too far and landed me with a ring through my belly button thanks to Carter's older sister. Cliché, maybe, but it looked hot. Anyone could see it if they happened to go swimming with me, or if I threw on a crop top, but the way she says it, you'd think it was somewhere even the tiniest of bikinis would still cover.

"Not yet."

She smirks, but there's no jealousy in it. No bitterness. And that's what makes it cruel. "It's only a matter of time, I'm sure."

"I guess." I still can't get past Shannon running to Jasmine after she spoke to me. I guess she had her phone number after all. "So you're talking to me now?"

"I haven't been not talking to you, Tinkerbell. We literally just talked at my party."

Tinkerbell. The resurgence of my nickname might suffuse me with warmth if she weren't giving me such attitude. But I was right, I realize—Jasmine *did* need to know that I wasn't going to try to bring things back to where they'd been this summer. She needed me to have a boyfriend in order for us to be friends, so she could be sure I wasn't going to pursue her. I'd been happy when I first thought of how maybe that would bring us back to normal, but right now it makes me feel sick.

"OK, whatever. Guess it doesn't matter since you've had no trouble making friends here." I try to keep my voice light, to remember how grateful I am for the friends she made me a few months ago, even if they fell to the wayside. But my feelings at her buddying up with Shannon drip from every word, and it doesn't help that I'm upset about the other stuff.

The thing is, I wanted us to be friends, and I wanted to date Chase, and it looks like I'm gonna get it all, so I *should* be happy. At the very least, I should be nice. "Guess this means you'll be joining us for lunch?"

"Shannon did mention something about that, yeah."

"Great!" I plaster a smile on my face. "Guess I'll see you then."

I walk off before she can leave me first.

It takes two periods before I finally have a class with Shannon, and as soon as I spot her, I storm over and demand, "What the fuck, Shan?"

"What's wrong?" she asks in the world's most bullshit innocent voice.

I yank her out into the hallway, because we're already drawing stares. "I told you about my date in confidence. You know there's nothing official between me and Chase yet. Why the hell would you run off and tell some girl you barely even know all about it?"

"God, Lara, I'm sorry. It sounded pretty official to me, and I was excited for you. I figured you'd want to tell Gia and Kiki, so when Jasmine called . . ." She shrugs. "I had to get my excitement out somehow!"

She is so full of shit. I *know* she's full of shit. For one, there's no chance Jasmine called her. Jasmine is *not* a phone person, and certainly not to chat. But I'm too deep into my own bullshit to be able to call her on that. I'm not supposed to know this, or anything else, about Jasmine.

Plus, I know this move from Shannon's playbook. Jasmine is on the popularity radar and Shannon's trying to swoop in so the next time someone asks for details on her love life or why she has such a nice house, Shannon can be The One With All The Dirt. "Knowledge Is Power" is one of Shannon Salter's favorite mottos, and it's hard to argue with since she sure seems to have a lot of the latter.

Unfortunately, I also know there's nothing I can do. Shannon always finds a way to spin things, to make it seem like she was just being a great friend in the best way she knows how; she's a gaslighting gold medalist. And the mere mention of Jasmine's name already feels like a minefield. There's no point in fighting here. Shannon's gonna do what she wants, and so will Jasmine. And fuck it, so will I.

"Whatever." I roll my eyes right as Mrs. Spier turns the corner, and I slip back into the classroom and into my seat before I can get called late.

Jasmine wants me to be with Chase. Shannon is apparently *very* excited I'm with Chase. And we all know *I* want to be with Chase. So, what exactly am I fighting about?

Maybe Chase and I aren't official yet, but by the end of our next date, we damn well will be.

And my summer with Jasmine will be a distant memory.

Chapter Seven

THEN

It's been three days of fruitful tanning and fruitless job
hunting when someone finally blocks out my sun. I look
up to see Jasmine standing over me, an impressive camera
bag slung over her shoulder. "Listen," she says without
preamble, because she doesn't believe in preamble. "My
dad feels really bad about screwing you out of a job, and
I could use an assistant this summer, so how do you feel
about helping me out a few days a week, all expenses
paid by Papa Dec?"

I shift slowly into a sitting position, trying to take this
in. Jasmine and I have barely spoken since the night of
the party. In fact, I've barely even seen her. It's only by
the grace of Keisha, Brea, and Derek that I've had anyone to hang out with at all.

Also, an assistant? For what? If she does anything
other than read, tan, and make out with Carter, it's

news to me. If she thinks I'm going to be carrying her bag around like she's some celebutante—

"I'm a photographer," she says, a little smile playing on her lips that makes it clear my confusion was obvious. "Well, I'm a web designer, but I'm building a stock photo portfolio as part of that. I've already gotten all the beach and bikini shots I can handle for the week, so I was thinking of heading down to the Elizabethan Gardens to get some flower shots. You in or not? I gotta go in the next half hour to get the right light."

There is suddenly a lot happening, but I'm bored as hell and I could use the money and company. Plus, the Elizabethan Gardens sound pretty, and I haven't done a single touristy thing since I got here other than check out a billion cheesy shops selling magnets shaped like flip-flops and wind chimes with surfboard charms. I take a quick shower and throw on cutoffs and a tank top, and we hit the road to Manteo.

Jasmine is not a woman of many words, and I'm trying not to be annoying though I have a zillion questions about her business, so all I learn on the twenty-minute drive is her favorite music—or at least whatever she listens to in the car—is all by bands I've never heard of: Chronic Apathy, the Pepperpots, Glory Alabama, the Brightsiders, and some group whose name I don't catch but who are definitely singing about wishing they were the scar on Padma Lakshmi's arm.

Once we're among the flowers, though, it's like she's a different person. As she sets up her shots, she explains to me how she can use some as background options for her website templates, and others might be used on book covers with other elements photoshopped in. She takes close-ups of brightly colored blooms and impossible shots of fluttering butterflies, and I'm so mesmerized watching her work, and how she seems to know the names of every blossom and creature, that I don't hear her the first time she says, "Jump in one."

The second time she says it, I immediately respond, "Nah, it's OK. I don't wanna get in your way." But truthfully, I do, because the background is gorgeous, and let's be real, I am not one to pass up a good profile pic.

Thankfully, she sees right through me, and before I can protest again, she yanks me over to a bench surrounded by fragrant patches of lilies and sits me down. "You know," she says, frowning in concentration as she fusses with my shoulder-length, nutmeg-colored mess, "I'm jealous. Your hair has so many possibilities. You could chop it to your chin and would look amazing, especially with a little curl."

"That's too much—I could never go that short," I say, though I'm already picturing it and I don't hate what I see.

"The summer's young," she says with a smile, stepping back and handing me a petal-pink lip gloss from her bag. "It's always a good time to get brave and make some fun changes."

I dab on the gloss and hand it back, patently ignoring the little chill of excitement at the thought of coming back to Stratford with a different look—one that wasn't advised, evaluated, and picked apart by my friends first. Then I smile, pout, and otherwise pose my way through a photo shoot with Jasmine mock-barking commands at me every time I move my limbs. "More duck face!" she demands, taking shot after shot of me pushing my lips up and out until they take up half my face. "More! Duckier! I said *duckier*!"

Eventually, we have to stop because I'm laughing too hard, and Jasmine goes back to taking her more official photos while I scramble to take light meter readings and rearrange stems.

After a couple of hours in the sweltering heat, I'm sweating like a pig and mentally begging for Jasmine to call it a day, but she doesn't seem to notice the temperature. There's no moisture beading on the skin above her tube top, and her flowy skirt dances as she moves, making it look like she's bringing her own breeze with her wherever she goes. Even the dark, honey-highlighted hair piled into a bun on top of her head isn't sticking to her face.

"Middle Eastern blood," she says with a shrug, and I curse my Russian DNA for leaving me unprepared. Next to her, I look like a panting sheepdog.

When she finally declares it's time to pack it in, I'm beyond relieved. I can already feel the air conditioning in her Jeep. But at four o'clock, there's plenty of daylight left, and I have no idea what to do with it. I want to ask, "Now what?" but she's already taken me under her wing for the day, and I imagine she must want some space.

Sure enough, there's no mention of evening plans on the way home, only twenty minutes of indie rock followed by "Thanks for the help" when we get out at her house. I'm halfway to my room when she says, "Owen's having some people over for a barbecue tonight, if you wanna come." Before I can answer, the main bathroom door shuts. A few seconds later, the shower turns on, and I realize she has completely taken my "yes" for granted.

God, I must radiate loneliness.

I take a shower in the smaller bathroom I share with my mom, then check the phone I've barely glanced at all day. There are a couple of pictures from Shannon on the group text chain—a selfie with a croissant between her teeth and a shot of her linking arms with a cute guy while drinking champagne—a video from Gia of her falling on her ass during a routine, and a notification that Kiki posted a new episode of her podcast. I smile at the latter and queue it up after posting my favorite selfie from the gardens, letting Kiki's familiar, soothing voice surround me as I moisturize.

"What is that?" a voice asks, and I nearly jump out of my towel when I realize Jasmine's standing in the doorway to our little suite. I hadn't realized I never closed the door, and now I'm standing here half naked, though thankfully only the two of us are home.

I wrap the towel tighter around myself and swipe at my face to clear any visible dabs of lotion. "My friend Kiki's podcast, *Kiki on the Case*. It's fun—it's like a gossip column where she plays detective, and she posts a new episode every week."

"Ooh, cute." Jasmine comes in and sits down on my bed, privacy clearly not a dominant word in her vocabulary. "What's this episode about?"

"Our school librarian is having kind of a dramatic breakup, and Kiki's a little obsessed with it," I say with a smile because it's so silly and so Kiki. "I mean, she didn't originally *say* it was our school librarian on the podcast, but we all know it is, because Ms. Adams is always on the phone in the library and she doesn't follow her own 'Shhh' very well. Rumor is she's hooking up with the librarian at our town's middle school, and Kiki's trying to confirm it, with the help of her little sister, who's in sixth grade."

"That . . . is bizarre."

"Isn't it?" God, I miss my friends. They're so weird. I have to remember to message them later about my new job and about how much I love this episode of the podcast; Kiki lives and dies by her fandom. "Kiki's obsessed with mysteries. It's her thing. She has to find out if it's really him so she can dig into how they met and what went wrong, because of course she does."

Jasmine laughs. "You should bring her to Roanoke."

"Roanoke? Isn't that in Virginia?"

"Different Roanoke. Haven't you ever learned about the lost colony in school? The settlers who disappeared?"

Oh, yeah, this is vaguely familiar. "I think so. Maybe."

"Guessing history is not your subject," Jasmine teases, and I confirm that it's definitely not. "Anyway, it was this whole thing in the late sixteenth century—the first attempt at a colony. These people came over from England, set up a town, and then . . . completely disappeared. Nothing left but a single word: CROATOAN. There are all sorts of theories about whether they were murdered or just moved to another place, but no one's ever been able to definitively say. There's a theater right near the gardens we were at today that does a show about it every night. I bet your friend would love it."

"Oh man, she would!" Bringing Kiki down here for a weekend sounds like a lot of fun, and there's no way a mystery like that isn't already super high on her radar. "Do you think your dad would let me have a friend here for a couple of days?"

Jasmine shrugs. "Sure, why not? If you're still gonna be here August 18, that's the day to go. It's silly, but they call it Virginia Dare Day. They even use a real baby in the show, in honor of Virginia Dare's birthday—she was the first new settler born on colonized soil. Garden admission is discounted that day, too, if you wanna take her there."

I actually don't know when we're heading back to New York. You'd think I'd be counting down the days, but right at this moment, I'm looking forward to going on some more adventures here. Seeing more stuff. Learning more from this girl who's full of surprises. "That's a cool idea, thank you."

She nods. "Sure. I'll leave you to get dressed."

The barbecue that night is a lot of fun, as is pizza and night swimming at Keisha's the evening after, and going to a Battle of the Bands at a club the night after that, and a sunset sail on Brea's boat the night after that. The days are cool too, even as Jasmine begins to trust me with heavier equipment and more work, leaving my muscles sore and my skin lobster-pink at the end of long days shooting lighthouses, slow-crawling crabs, and hang gliders. I get to see everything touristy from a completely different angle, and I always expect Jasmine to mock the cheesy gift shops and fanny packs, but she never does. Instead, she plays the role of tour guide, adding her own little-known facts about the first flights to our stroll around the Wright Brothers Memorial and the histories of the different lighthouses. It's clear that coming to the Outer Banks for summers her entire life has given her a profound pride in the place.

I've never seen someone find so much beauty in everything.

But by Friday night, which brings us to a poker game at Carter's, she seems wiped. She doesn't acknowledge it as she drives us to his house, though. She's just quiet, the way she is to and from photo shoots, a time I've come to realize she uses to go over her plans in her head. But unless she's planning card strategies, that isn't what's on her mind.

I don't push. Something tells me that never works with her.

"How real is this poker game?" I ask instead. I brought it up to distract her, but I'm a little nervous. "Is this, like, playing for M&Ms, or for actual cash? Because I don't have a whole lot of the latter."

She waves her hand. "I know. Don't worry about it. I'll spot you."

Okay, I'm annoyed. It's enough that I'm living in her house, well aware my mom is her dad's secretary and I'm her "assistant." I don't need to be handed out cash favors. "I'm not looking to be spotted; I want to be prepared."

"You'll be fine" is all she says, and now I'm silent too, irritated at her new clothes and this fancy Jeep and how she's probably gone to shows for every one of these stupid bands on her stupid satellite radio. But then she follows it up with, "Here, why don't you pick the music? Put on whatever helps you de-stress."

I do not need to be asked twice to blast Demi Lovato.

It turns out the buy-in is fifty bucks, which I don't have. But I offer to help Carter in the kitchen, shoving trays of frozen pigs in a blanket and mozzarella sticks in the oven as slowly as I can to avoid the question of whether I'm going to be up-front about not having the money, or do something stupid like promise to pay Jasmine back so I can not embarrass myself in front of my new friends.

But when all the food is in and I've stirred the lemonade for so long I've probably churned it into butter, I'm out of time.

When I finally enter the game room (yeah, he has a game room), Carter says, "Hey, Jasmine's low on cash this week, so we're doing a buy-in at ten. That cool?"

I shrug, forcing myself to meet his eyes so I don't have to look anywhere near hers. "Sure."

Turns out, I am not very good at poker—not at bluffing, nor remembering that a flush is a thing, nor reading other people's facial expressions. But Jasmine is wiping the floor with everyone. I should've known she'd be great at it. She has the best poker face I've ever seen. I've picked up slight frowns and nose wrinkles I thought must indicate crappy cards, but nope. Inside of an hour, she has everyone's money, including mine, and shockingly, nobody feels like playing another round.

"I knew I should've let your invite get lost in the mail," Carter teases, but it's obvious from the way he's looking at her that it's everyone else's invites he would've rather lost instead. I expect Jasmine to flirt and it to take point-twelve seconds for them to head off to his room, but all she says is, "Better luck next time, sucker," as her long, ring-laden fingers proceed to shuffle the cards like a pro.

We drink hard cider and play Asshole until Jack and Derek disappear to fool around and Owen and Brea head to a party on the beach, and it's me and Jasmine, Keisha, and Carter left.

The wingwoman handbook dictates that Keisha and I GTFO, but she doesn't appear to be in a rush to go anywhere. Instead, she takes the deck from where it was abandoned during the rush of cheek-kiss goodbyes and gives it a shuffle worthy of Vegas. It's starting to feel like I'm the only one here not born with an ace up her sleeve and a joker in every pocket. "Spades?" she suggests, cracking her cinnamon gum, but judging from the way Carter and Jasmine seamlessly shift around the table to split us into teams—cousins versus housemates—it isn't really a suggestion.

This is confirmed when I reach for a second cider, only to feel Jasmine's rings dig into my wrist. "You're gonna need to keep your wits about you, Tinkerbell," she warns me. "These two share a Spades brain."

I snort. "I think I can handle it."

I could not, in fact, handle it. "The two of you are such shitty cheaters!" I yelp after getting utterly destroyed for a third hand in a row. "This is not humanly possible."

Keisha smiles smug and wide, tossing her tight

beaded braids over shoulder, while Carter throws back his head and laughs. "We've been coming down here since we were babies," she says, her Southern accent coming in stronger as the night wears on and the alcohol settles in. "Carter's brother and our cousin Richie trained us at this table as soon as we could walk."

"There's not a lot to do here after dark before you get a driver's license," Carter confirms. "At least not before I discovered girls."

"You mean before girls discovered *you*," Keisha says with a snort. "Your goofy ass wasn't exactly 'filling the time' until you came back six inches taller and with your braces off."

"Burrrrrn," I say instinctively before realizing that Jasmine is one of those girls, though she seems completely unbothered. In fact, she's laughing too. I turn to Keisha, remembering that she mentioned being aroace. "And what'd you do while girls were 'discovering' Carter? Guessing you had . . . different preoccupations."

"Slightly," she says with a laugh, dealing another hand. "I'm a gaming nerd, so I was plenty happy to stay home while Carter and them went out, play *The Sims* or *Dragon Age* until sunrise. But lots of nights we all stayed in and played, same as we did waiting up for Santa when we were kids."

"See, *that's* my problem," says Jasmine, tugging on the six-pointed star charm hanging at her throat. "Too Jewish."

"Hey, me too!" I cheer, and we slap five over the table while they laugh. My mom and I aren't remotely affiliated—the one thing we do all year is light menorahs and eat latkes on the first night of Hanukkah, which we only do because it makes my mom feel better about raising me on Christmas—but it feels like the first thing we've had in common.

Except for how we both suck at Spades.

But it's fun, and Jasmine seems so much more at ease in the smaller crowd. It takes the sting out of losing so badly to see her chilled out, more like the person I hang out with on photo shoots and long car drives. By the time we officially bite the dust, my face hurts from laughing so hard. At least until Carter asks us to stick around, his eyes hovering somewhere around Jasmine's lips, and my stomach drops at the thought of ending our fun night by being ditched.

"Nah. We've gotta get up early for a sunrise shoot," says Jasmine, rising on her toes to give him a peck on the cheek. The shoot is news to me, but I nod and accept good-night hugs and promises of a rematch. Keisha and I even exchange numbers, and I appreciate that her phone case is designed to look like a vintage Nintendo controller.

"Are we really doing a sunrise shoot tomorrow?" I ask after we buckle ourselves in and leave the Thomases behind us.

"Sure, why not?" Jasmine shrugs. "People love cheesy sunrises for social media backgrounds and templates. Unless you don't think you can get up that early."

I've been getting up early to run on the beach the past couple days, before Jasmine or Mom or even Declan is awake. It's been nice having time to myself where I'm not in Declan's house, or assisting Jasmine, or tiptoeing around my mom. I've never been a morning person, but running on the sand is more relaxing than walking on eggshells and feeling like an interloping piece of luggage my mom was forced to bring.

I don't wanna give up my secret, though. "Oh, I can. The question is whether you want company that early. You don't seem to enjoy the presence of others before coffee."

Her teeth flash in the dark interior of the car. "You've noticed."

"I'm very observant," I say with a flip of my hair.

"You are." Her voice is more serious than I anticipate, and I'm not ready for it. "I like this about you. You know when to talk and when not to. It's a rare skill."

"I'll take that as a compliment." It strikes me then that it's the first time we've driven without music. "Especially since you can be a hard girl to read."

The corner of her mouth turns up. "Not many people bother to try to read me."

Outside, it's relatively quiet, and with our windows down, we can hear the ocean lapping at the shore during the pauses in our conversation. The peaceful rhythmic interlude makes it less glaring that it takes me a minute to figure out how to respond.

"I don't know about that. We just left a whole house of people sick of losing to you at poker."

She laughs. "Touché. But none of them like to work for it."

"Have you ever considered not making people work for it?"

"Literally never."

"Well, at least you're self-aware."

My phone beeps, and I know before I look down that it's gonna be my mom, asking where we are. I quickly tap out that we'll be home in two minutes, and Jasmine says, "I didn't really make *you* work for it, did I?"

I think of how quickly she invited me to the pool, to meet her friends, to join in on her photo shoots. I press send on my reply and say, "No, you didn't, I suppose." Although all of that was superficial; there's still so much I don't know. But I like the idea that I'm a standout. What can I say? I'm vain. "Am I just special?"

Her lips twitch. "I guess you are."

"I *feel* special," I say seriously. It's meant to sound like teasing, but I do. I'm grateful for how much she's helped me love it here, for how generous she's been with her time, with her life. Hell, I'm even grateful that she listened to me tonight about not wanting to be spotted and found another way to make it work. "To what do I owe the honor?"

"You really wanna know?"

"Obviously."

She pulls us into the driveway and shuts off the car. "You cut through bullshit really, really fast. I cannot even tell you how refreshing that is."

I definitely owe that to a combination of my mom, who has zero time for bullshit, and Shannon, who taught me not to bother since she'll see right through me anyway. But I don't feel like giving anyone else credit. I'm enjoying feeling special—unnervingly so. I'm not gonna say that either, so instead I deflect like the wind. "Well, as long as I'm doing that: I thought you'd want to stay longer tonight. Hang out with Carter." I let the rest go unsaid.

She glances at me, her usually golden eyes impenetrably dark. "Can I tell you something, only because I think you'll get it and not think I'm extremely weird?"

I have no idea what's coming, but there's only one right answer to that question. "Of course."

There's a tear in the thigh of her jeans, and she picks at it, concentrating her gaze downward with the same intensity she gives to capturing perfect shots of butterflies. "I don't really love the whole partying thing. I mean, sometimes I do. But being surrounded by people is just . . . a lot. And it's not that I don't like hooking up with Carter, but it's like . . . I don't *need* it in the same way when there aren't a ton of people there."

My first thought is that she means she wants other people to see it. After all, how many times have I dreamed of the feeling of a million eyes on me as I stand with Chase under the spotlight at Homecoming or prom? But that isn't the vibe I get from Jasmine. And then I *do* get it.

"You don't need the escape, you mean?"

The smile on her lips is faint, but I see it because I'm looking for it. "Yeah."

It isn't something we have in common. I like to be kept busy, to be surrounded, entertained. As much as I love my mom, I suspect it's from growing up in a quiet house of two. But sometimes always having to be "on," having to abide by Shannon's "rules," having to balance school and work and, yeah, even my high-maintenance crush can get exhausting and frustrating and I just want that feeling of taking your bra off at the end of the day more than I want anything else in the world.

Even if it feels like I'm not allowed to admit it.

"So why do you keep going out?"

She shrugs. "I don't wanna be alone either. There's no real compromise here—you either hang out with everyone, or no one."

"Well," I say, a brilliant idea sparking in my brain, "maybe that was true before, but it isn't now. *Now* you have a housemate! How about tomorrow night we stay back and hang out? We can have an incredibly cheesy and stereotypical girls' night. Heavy on the ice cream. Hair curlers optional."

Jasmine laughs with a rare fullness that I'm way too proud of eliciting. "Deal."

We shake hands before going inside.

I think about that handshake a lot, because it reassures me that it was clearly just a friendly suggestion.

I had no idea what it would spark.

Chapter Eight

NOW

There was a time when I always put up with Shannon's shit because it was easier than fighting with her, but it turns out that was completely pointless—I've been mad all week, and she doesn't even notice. When I grunt in response to her questions or bail on lunch to work on a lab report, she acts like that's nothing out of the ordinary and goes on chattering about the shopping trip she's taking with her mom in SoHo for her birthday and this guy she hooked up with in France who keeps sending her pictures of himself making sad faces over missing her.

I try to make eyes with Kiki and Gia, but as usual, Gia's hanging on every word and piping up with ways Tommy either is or should be more romantic, and Kiki couldn't care less, because some huge YouTuber named *Kiki on the Case* as his newest bonkers obsession. She's managing a wild increase in followers and subscribers, so her only contributions to conversations this week have been things like "What do you think about a series on celebrity death conspiracy theories, starting with Marilyn Monroe? I need to appeal to a bigger audience now."

I *would* be thrilled when things are shaken up with a new face at our lunch table on Friday, except that face belongs to Jasmine.

"Yay!" Shannon claps her hands together as Jasmine takes a seat, setting down a tray of chicken fingers and tater tots with extra hot sauce. "Excited you finally made it."

Finally made it? Ugh. If I weren't already annoyed at Shannon, knowing she's been inviting Jasmine to lunch every damn day would certainly do it. Shannon only tries this hard with people when she thinks they have something of value to add to our group. I wonder whether it was Jasmine's gorgeous house or killer party that did it. Both are sort of weird options, since Shannon has every bit as nice a house, and plenty of kids around here throw good parties, but what else could it be? It's not like she knows that Jasmine has gorgeous photography skills and amazing taste in books, or that she's the most fun person to road-trip with because she'll howl the most ridiculous lyrics out the window and make up the best and most filthy backstories for strangers in the cars next to us. And I'm reasonably certain she doesn't know that Jasmine is an excellent kisser.

Does she?

Suddenly, my own tater tots look way less appealing.

I grab a cucumber slice from my salad and nibble that instead.

"It's been a busy week," says Jasmine with all the apology in her voice she can muster, which frankly isn't much. "It's not exactly the same curriculum as in Asheville. I have to catch up on some stuff."

"Why did you move for senior year again?" Kiki asks, and I can practically see antennae rise out of her messy bun.

"Custody stuff," Jasmine says as if it's nothing, like being shuffled between parents at a whim doesn't bother her, but it's bullshit. There's no way she isn't missing her mom's lavish Shabbat dinners. There's no way she feels at home in a bedroom with no pictures on the walls.

But everyone else accepts it with a nod—a slightly disappointed one, in Kiki's case—and she bites into a chicken finger while motioning "Can't possibly speak on this further as my mouth is currently full."

"Well, you have perfect timing for joining us," says Shannon, "because our little Larissa is going on a big date tonight, and I wanna hear all about it." Her lips twitch into the tiniest of smirks. "I'm allowed to reveal that now, right?"

Fucker. She did know I was pissed all week.

I don't need Jasmine knowing how bothered I am by their random-ass friendship, nor am I letting Shannon win this one. "Duh. About fifty people already asked me about it today, so." Insert modest shrug, as if I don't know that the idea of me and Chase being the center of Stratford conversation drives her nuts. "I'm glad we

decided to just see a movie instead of going out in public. Who needs all those eyes on us?"

"A movie," Jasmine says sweetly. "That sounds . . .
romantic."

Is she trying to make me feel the weight of her hand
on my thigh, the way it pressed my skin into the scratchy
velvet of the movie theater seat? Because it's definitely
not working.

"Ooh, especially at the multiplex," says Gia. "They
have those reclining seats that are so big, they can fit
two people. It's *very* romantic," she adds in a tone that
makes me want to bring bleach to the theater.

"So, start from the beginning," says Jasmine, smiling
like this is normal girl talk and she's enjoying it and
aren't we all enjoying it? "How did he ask? What are you
wearing?"

"You still have my really cute halter," Shannon points
out, as if my favorite blue tank top isn't buried somewhere in the depths of her walk-in closet. "It's so cute
with jeans."

"Jeans are so boring!" Gia protests. "Jasmine, tell her
she has to wear a dress."

"I have some cute dresses you can borrow." Jasmine's
voice is light and playful and a flush starts creeping up
my skin. I'm familiar with her cute dresses. I've bor-
rowed a couple that don't require her considerably more
ample cleavage. And I know exactly which ones give
easy access in a movie theater too.

I hate this conversation. I hate that she's here. I hate
that my brain won't let this summer go.

I hate that I don't know if she's thinking the same

things I am or if the offer to borrow a dress is really just an offer to borrow a dress.

"Thanks, but I think Shannon's right about the halter and jeans," I say, my words coming out in a mumble. "Don't wanna give him any ideas just yet, right?" I don't know what I'm talking about anymore.

"Right," Gia says. "Make him work for it. I wouldn't even let Tommy touch my boobs for three months."

"We know, G," Kiki says on a huffy sigh, refreshing something on her phone screen. "We know."

"What are you doing besides a movie?" Jasmine asks, resting her chin on her palm. "Are you going out to dinner too? Or just gonna make out in his car a lot?"

The other girls laugh, and I can't tell if it's mean-spirited, on her end or on theirs. I don't know how to feel about any of this except that I want Jasmine to stop asking me stupid fucking questions about my date with Chase.

The truth is that I haven't really thought about it. Despite a movie date with Chase being item number four on my high school bucket list, I'm not obsessing; I'm just plain old looking forward. I'd picked an outfit (yes, I'd already been planning on wearing the halter top and jeans before Shannon ever opened her mouth), and I'd let my mom know I was going out and might be a little late, but would text her before curfew.

It's a movie. What more is there to say about a movie?

A lot, apparently.

Well, if that's the game Jasmine wants to play.

"I'm pretty sure there'll be plenty of making out wherever we go. Who's got time for dinner when

Chase Harding is on the menu?" I flash a sly smile and take a sip of my Diet Coke while the other girls whistle and laugh. I'm gratified to see Jasmine purse her lips a little bit, just enough to know she's done with the question portion of our meal. "What are the rest of you doing tonight?"

In the end, I wear a short red skirt with a black-and-white polka dot top—neither Shannon's suggestion, nor Jasmine and Gia's—and I don't give a damn what ideas Chase gets; I'll do what I want. I also wear red lipstick, even though Shannon's told me a million times that it scares guys off from kissing you, and the black leather sandals she once told me to burn because they made me look stumpy. (They make my legs look athletic, thank you very much.)

Judging from the look on Chase's face when I answer the door, I look just fine. Better than. Or, if I wasn't sure, his "Wow, you look gorgeous" helps.

"Thanks," I say, accepting a kiss on the cheek. I call back to my mom that I'm heading out and wait until I hear her "Have fun!" before following him out to his car.

There's no movie theater in Stratford, but the multiplex with the awesome seats is only a fifteen-minute drive, so we buckle in and make small talk about school and the movie's reviews and work and the football team. More than once, I catch him checking me out at a red light, and by the time we get to the theater, I'm bursting to ask him the thing that's been bothering me since the first day of school.

"Hey, can I ask you a weird question?"

He shuts off the engine. "How weird are we talking?"

"It's . . . you've known for a while that I like you, right?" I can't believe the words coming out of my mouth. "Like, it hasn't exactly been the best-kept secret at Stratford."

He grins, and I wish the overhead light hadn't gone off so I could see him in better light. "A little while, maybe. But I like you too."

"Yeah, I got that," I say, and we both laugh. "I guess I'm just wondering . . . why now? Is it really the haircut? The blond? I hope it's not the tan, because that's already on its way out."

"Those things don't hurt," he says, reaching out to lightly yank a golden curl, "but no, it isn't that you're prettier than before. You just seem different. You kinda . . . glow. I mean, you walked into school that first day straight-up strutting." He laughs, more sheepishly this time. "God, that sounds dumb. But do you know what I mean? You seem happier, a little more fearless, a little less like . . ."

"Like . . . ?"

"I'm trying to figure out how to say this in a way that doesn't sound awful."

My stomach tightens. "Well, it can't sound worse than this."

"Fair enough." He meets my gaze full-on, his eyes glowing with the reflection of the neon lights. "You seem less like you're in Shannon Salter's shadow. Like you somehow came into your own this summer. If that's not a really stupid and terrible thing to say."

I shake my head slowly. "It isn't either of those things." I hadn't really put it into those words, but I think I felt some of that too.

The only problem was that sure, I hadn't spent the summer in Shannon's shadow, but maybe I'm in Jasmine's shadow. Only no one knows it.

Jasmine is the one who inspired my haircut, who gave me the bravery for my piercing. Jasmine is the one who took me all over the Outer Banks, showed me how to find beauty in places I didn't see it, including— cheesy as it is—myself. Jasmine is the one who showed me the real fun was never in following the crowd, and that sometimes the best things are the scary and the unexpected.

God, a part of me hates her so much.

But it hits me with a bolt that what Chase is seeing is that I love *myself* more after this summer, and for that, I will probably owe her forever.

"Good," he says, and it isn't until he says it that I remember where I am and who I'm with. "So, should we get some popcorn?"

THEN

We did hang out by ourselves the night after the poker game, but there was no ice cream; instead, we stocked up on graham crackers, Hershey bars, and marshmallows, and made good use of the fire pit in the backyard.

"What do you think happens if you leave a marshmallow in a bottle of soda?" Jasmine asks, holding up one of the many bottles of Coke we'd bought to accompany our s'mores, determined to taste test every one of its sweet varieties. "Do you think it explodes?"

"Uh-oh. Do you think having both in our stomachs at the same time will make *them* explode?"

Jasmine laughs and whacks me on the arm. "Shut up! This is serious. We should experiment. For science."

"For science, you want to waste a perfectly good marshmallow by dropping it into a bottle of cherry Coke."

"Would you prefer I waste a perfectly good marshmallow by dropping it into a bottle of orange vanilla?"

"Don't you dare. Orange vanilla's my favorite." I grab the bottle of carbonated Creamsicle and chug it while using my other hand to throw a marshmallow square at Jasmine's nose.

"*Now* who's wasting a perfectly good marshmallow, Larissa?"

The combination of her using my full name and her mock-angry tone cracks me up, and my sugar high doesn't help. This is so gross but also so delicious, and even without everybody else, even though we already spent the whole day together going through pictures and analyzing tedious details to pick the best shots, this is the most fun night I've had since we came down here.

"You're such a dork," I say, grabbing stuff to make another s'more. "But I'm glad we stayed in. It's nice to chill out and wear comfy clothes and let my hair get all rat's nest-y."

She laughs. "Your hair is not rat's nest-y, but yeah, isn't it? Like, it's fun to hang out with other people, but it all becomes about the same shit—everyone just wants to feel good at the end of the night, right? You get drunk to feel good. You hook up to feel good. You take other people's money at the poker table to feel good. And it's so much fucking work." The smile has slid off her lips, and her face grows serious in the light of the fire, the sparks reflecting in her amber eyes. "It doesn't have to be so much work. It doesn't have to be constantly making sure you're wearing the right thing, saying the right thing, drinking the right amount, worrying about who's watching you do what.

"Sometimes it's so fucking exhausting to feel good that it doesn't even feel good when it should. We act like beer and boys are so necessary for a good time, for a *real* night, and honestly, fuck that. If all we cared about was making out with someone—" I've barely swallowed my s'more and suddenly there are lips on mine, sweet with a trace of chocolate. Only a moment, and then the cool night air rushes in off the water again, as if it never happened. "Just . . . do it. You don't have to throw a whole massive party so three hours later you can get someone back to your room to make out. Just *make out*. The whole pretense is so tired. I wish people would just admit what they want when they want it."

I'm not sure I've blinked once her whole tirade. I definitely haven't moved since her lips landed on mine. What the hell just happened?

Suddenly, her face crumbles, every trace of righteous

indignation gone. "Oh, shit, Lara, I'm sorry. I got caught up. I shouldn't have done that. I promise I—"

"Shh." I hold up a hand, silencing her, as I think about years of wanting Chase. Years of going to his football games and the parties afterward. Yeah, they were fun, but ultimately, what did I want? I wanted him to notice me. I wanted him to want to be with me. I wanted to make out with him and have fun and feel good and lather rinse repeat until . . . what? Until I didn't want that anymore? I didn't have visions of us getting married and having babies. I had visions of him asking me to go upstairs at Ferris's house so we could make out.

For that, I had worn uncomfortable shoes and too-tight jeans and pounds of makeup and scorched my hair into perfect straightness and listened to Shannon tell me how to stand and what to smell like and what shades of lipstick I should wear.

All that, when sometimes it's as simple as s'mores and Coke and leaning over in your Adirondack chair on the beach.

I look at Jasmine—really look—at the trace of melted marshmallow on her lip and the apprehension in her eyes and a freckle on her shoulder and then I'm the one leaning over and doing the kissing, tasting sweet artificial cherry on her tongue and feeling so damn good in this moment we didn't work for.

It's so good that I don't realize we're falling out of our chairs until we land on the sand, our laughter floating into the summer night amid the crackling flames until our mouths find each other again and there's no more laughing at all.

NOW

"Lara? Hey." A gentle, masculine hand lands on my shoulder. "Did you want butter?"

Chapter Nine

NOW

"I think I got it this time!"

"You said that about the last one," Beth calls from where she's taking inventory of the mystery/thriller/suspense section. "It looked like a toddler's handprint at best."

"Hey, I'm new at this!" I scrutinize the leaf pattern I've drawn in the foam of my fourth cappuccino of the morning, and it definitely looks better than the other three. "A little support would be nice."

"A few more hours spent watching those YouTube videos would be nice," she mutters, but the store's empty except for us, and I hear every word. I've been trying to up my barista game by watching videos on drawing foam art, hoping to impress Beth with hearts and leaves and butterflies. Unfortunately, I'm about as good at doing art with foam as I am at doing it with paint, charcoal, decoupage, pencils, or anything else—which is to say, not at all.

The only thing I have to show for my training is a pair of slightly jittery hands from quickly downing my first two mistakes. (Beth graciously took the third, despite it being many shades lighter than her soul.) Latte art looks easy on YouTube, but so do makeup tutorials, and I suck at those too.

For as good a time as I had this summer, I can't help being resentful that I was forced to give up my bookseller position for something I suck at. I know books. I love books. I could've helped a bunch of dads find graphic novels for their daughters, could've pointed out the best romance novels for other sappy readers in search of humor and kissing, could've learned so much more about all the other books on the shelves—the awesomely titled "cozy mysteries," as Beth taught me they're called, or the zillions of young adult fantasies with crowns or swords on the covers. Working here isn't just about money—I want to learn how to do this, to be Beth, to one day surround myself with books and coffee and people who love both while working on my own romance novels in my downtime. I don't know exactly what I want to do with my life, but I do know I feel the closest to figuring it out when I'm here.

The best I can do now is prove that I can go above and beyond in whatever job I'm given, or at least I'll try to.

So in the eight minutes I have left until the store opens, I take Beth's muttered advice and get another instructional video going while I finish morning prep. I'm so wrapped up watching a pair of hands draw a swan that the first customer has to cough to get my attention. I offer my apologies and ask for her order, hoping it'll be a latte or a cappuccino or even a hot chocolate to give me another chance to practice, but like most of the customers clinging to the end of summer, she orders an iced coffee, and the only thing I can show off is that I can make one without screwing up. She also orders a mixed-berry scone, the café's most popular baked good (and the secret recipe of none other than Beth's nephew, Winston, whom I've never met but lives in Beth's basement and apparently has a golden touch with flour, sugar, eggs, and butter). I wrap it in the store's trademark lavender tissue paper, hand it over along with the iced coffee, and make change . . . only to say goodbye and see Jasmine Killary standing at the front of the line.

"Good morning and welcome to the Book and Bean," I greet her as if I'm not at all rattled by her presence, by her bedhead and lip gloss and the Bathory Belles concert T-shirt she wore the day we went to the Pea Island Wildlife Refuge and came back covered in bug bites. We spent the night soothing ourselves in the hot tub. "What can I get you?"

She glances at the chalk menu over my head. "What do you recommend?"

"Something with foam. I've been working on my art."

"Ooh, interesting." She taps her chin, showing off a plum-colored fingernail speckled with gold glitter. "Can you draw a puppy?"

"Probably as well as I can draw a leaf or a heart."

Her lips curve into a smile. "I'll have a puppy cappuccino, please, with a shot of vanilla."

I'm grateful for the opportunity to turn away from her and focus on the machinery. I need to concentrate on not burning myself on the steam wand and on swirling the milk just right, not on sniffing her honeysuckle shampoo.

Espresso fills the small café with a bitter scent that obliterates the honey teasing my nose, and I inhale deeply. I'm two steps from giving Jasmine her coffee and watching her leave when she says, "Hey, is that a flyer for a Clementine Walker event? How much did you have to beg to make that happen?"

Ah, so we're back to acknowledging we know each other, then. Okay. "A happy coincidence," I say, carefully pouring in the milk.

"Well, I'm curious to meet the legend herself. Shame it's not for another month. I'll have to put it into my calendar."

Is she screwing with me? She's gonna come to the Clementine Walker event? I can't tell if she's trying to ruin it for me or if this is a genuine attempt to be friends. But I don't have time to gauge it because the dad who loved my graphic novel recommendations appears right behind her.

Judging from the bounce in his step, I'm guessing the last round went well.

And Jasmine is going to hear all about it unless I can get her out of here.

"That'll be $5.26," I tell Jasmine, pushing her drink forward.

She squints at the top. "That's supposed to be a puppy? Really?"

Dammit, I forgot to be fancy with the top. Then again, it doesn't look much different than if I'd actually tried, judging by my earlier attempts. "What, you don't see it? There's the nose right there."

She raises an eyebrow but doesn't say anything. She hands over her credit card—*of course* she has her own—which reads Jasmine H Killary in crisp letters. The H stands for Helene. I hate that I know that.

"You draw puppies in the coffee now?" Graphic Novel Dad pipes up from behind Jasmine. "I'll have one of those too, please. And some more book recommendations if you've got 'em! I'm picking up the new Candy Buttons book today, but she goes through these so fast, I have to find something new."

So much for getting Jasmine out of here.

There's an unreadable look on her face as she says, "They have Candy Buttons? I may have to go pick up the new one myself."

"They have a great graphic novel section here since this one started," he says with a nod in my direction. I suddenly find myself very busy with literally anything but meeting Jasmine's gaze. "She helped me find some great books for my daughter, and I'm sure she'd be happy to help you too."

"I'll check out what there is first," she says, taking back her card. "Thanks for this."

I make a choked sound in response as I watch her head off to see that I've had Beth stock the store with every single one of her favorites, every book she passed to me that I fell in love with, every book I knew would find fans if we carried it.

I make the dad's drink and chat with him about some other choices for his daughter—*Mooncakes* and *This One Summer* and *I am Alfonso Jones*, recommendations I found on book blogs and promptly devoured—while I brace myself for Jasmine's return.

He leaves before she gets back, and her drink goes cold. I help myself to a few sips of it and make her a new one with shaking fingers, art and all. It's my worst design of the day, no question, but when she comes back to the counter with a smile on her lips, I have a feeling she won't mind. "That's a nice selection you have there." She glances at the coffee and laughs. "And a nice . . . spider?"

"I'm new at this," I mutter.

"Well, thank you for the new coffee. And for the books. You even have some I haven't tried yet; I'm gonna go ahead and buy a few."

"Great."

"Great indeed." She picks up her cup and tips it lightly in my direction with a "Bye, Tinkerbell" that sends a tremor through my knees.

Or maybe it's the caffeine.

After spending the whole morning standing over the steam of the cappuccino machine, an afternoon at Kiki's pool is exactly what I need. My hair is a mess of frizz and even in all black, you can see the zillion places I spilled coffee and foam on myself today. I call my messy self out before the others can beat me to it and change into one of the bathing suits I keep at Kiki's, because where else do I really need them now?

"Thank *God* it's still warm enough to sit by the pool," says Gia, ever dramatic as she stretches out on a floating raft, trailing her fingers in the water.

"Barely," I say miserably, stretching my legs out from my seat on the second-highest step. "I can feel my tan fading already." It's impossible to shake the concern that every little change I went through this summer has contributed to Chase's attraction, and even though it would make him a colossal ass if it were true, and even though he already said it isn't about how I look, I can't help feeling like if I shed too much of the summer, he'll realize I'm the same girl he wasn't interested in last year or the year before that.

"You can always join me at the salon," Gia singsongs. She is the queen of spray tans and is always trying to convince us to come along, but I just can't get on board. I would end up leaving splotches of orange on white surfaces all over town.

"Not gonna happen, G," says Shannon, slathering on another layer of sunscreen at the mere mention of tans. "Painting your skin is weird."

Kiki, who's Japanese American and naturally darker than the rest of us, just snorts and does a somersault in the pool.

"You're all gonna change your minds when it comes time to buy homecoming dresses," Gia warns.

"Speak for yourself," says Shannon. "I am wearing red lipstick and it's gonna look perfect with my paleness, thank you very much."

"How do you know what you're wearing already? We haven't even gone shopping yet," I say. I haven't given a ton of thought to Homecoming this year, but I've imagined myself on Chase's arm at it enough in the past. The dress is always nebulous, though—I like clothes, but being on a tight budget means shopping always feels like a mixed bag, for fear I'll find something I absolutely love that I can't take home in a million years.

It was a double-edged sword shopping with Jasmine— she knew my limitations, and like that night at the poker game, she never acknowledged them out loud; she just made sure we went to places that'd work for me. It was uncomfortable in its own way, but it didn't have that overhang of dread that shopping with Shannon did, the worry that she'd find something she thought looked so good on me she'd say "Just pay me back later" or "You have your mom's card—who cares if it's a little over budget?" And I couldn't get mad when she was trying to be nice. It wasn't her fault she was spoiled and completely clueless. But I couldn't exactly get mad at my mom either. All it left me with was a lot of frustration that usually had me going home with a headache.

This year, though . . . this year I have a date. *The* date. Chase hasn't officially asked me yet, but we'd had a good time the night before, and he'd asked me out again for the next weekend. He wouldn't ask me out again and *not* ask me to the second biggest dance of the year that was only a month from now, would he?

I lift my face to the sun, just in case.

"Some of us don't pull off every single color," says Gia with a sniff, as if I should somehow feel bad that green doesn't make me look sick the way it does to her, and white looks good as long as I've gotten some sun, the way it never would on Shannon. "We have to do some advance planning."

"Speaking of advance planning," says Shannon, "has Chase asked you yet? You were *very* stingy on date details last night."

She's referring to the group text that went on for half an hour after I got home, and she's full of crap because I told them everything from how much of the movie we spent making out (at least half) to what snacks we got (popcorn with extra butter and Milk Duds—he's a man of taste) to his exact wording when he asked me out for the next weekend ("I had a great time tonight—do you maybe wanna hang out again after the game next Friday?") But she's right that I didn't say anything about Homecoming, because it never came up.

Maybe it's more of a third date conversation?

"I can't believe you went on a date with Chase Harding and you're not talking about it nonstop." Kiki sends a delicate splash in my direction. "Who even are you? This is like the only thing you've wanted for six years."

Is it? God, that's sad. If you ask me what I want now, it's so many things—to learn how to sail, to show everyone my newfound poker skills, to spend a Sunday taking pictures at the botanical garden, to make perfect latte art, to meet Clementine Walker, to get my bookselling job back, to maybe even finish writing that romance novel someday.

But these girls don't know any of that. They know I like to party. They know I'm a dependable listener when it comes to relationship drama and a good roller coaster buddy and I find great discounts. That I like movie nights where we wear face masks and throw popcorn at each other, and that I can quote every word of my favorites (and that those favorites include everything from the fluffiest rom-com to the goriest horror flick). They know I'm a good shopping buddy, and the one you turn to if you need help with an English assignment. That if we go into the city on a weekend, I'm gonna push to eat at my favorite Russian restaurant. And all of that is true. It is who I am. Who I've always been.

But now I know I'm all this other stuff too, and I certainly don't wanna be first and foremost the Girl Obsessed with Chase Harding.

Except I *was* the girl obsessed with Chase Harding, so where has that obsession gone, now that we're finally together? Was it only the thrill of the chase (pun not intended), or is there more to it?

How do you tell your closest friends, when you only have one year left before you all head off in new directions, that they don't know you as well as they think?

How do you have that conversation when it means facing that *you* didn't know yourself as well as you thought you did?

I close my eyes and think of all the things I've told these girls in the past—my first period, my first kiss, my first Father's Day rage cry, my first "oh my God, I am helplessly in love with this boy."

Telling them something has always been what makes it real.

Maybe I'm not ready for that yet.

No, not maybe—I am definitely not ready for that.

"There'll be more," I say to assure them and myself,

letting the sun warm my skin. "Don't worry, you'll have to hear about each and every one."

The other girls boo, and Kiki splashes much less delicately in my direction. And I smile.

Monday at lunch, though, boys are anything but the topic of discussion. At some point over the weekend—between movie dates, lounging at the pool, and another morning spent drawing bad leaves in lattes—college fever swept the entire town of Stratford. It might be because early decision deadlines are nearing, or because Homecoming is the *other* thing on everyone's mind and people are about to return from all over, anxious to tell us how much they looooove their schools and prying like mad about where we're going, but whatever it is, Shannon, Kiki, and Gia have come armed to our centrally located table today.

"Obviously I'm still applying to Columbia," says Shannon, "but I can't *not* consider the Sorbonne, especially after spending the summer in Paris. I'll apply to Brown too, but I mean, Providence? Really?"

Kiki rolls her eyes into her Coke. She drinks like seven cups of it a day, even after our science lab where we watched it take the rust off a nail. "Brown's a great school, Shan. I would apply there if they had a forensic science program, or a journalism major."

"Are you *sure* you want to center your early decision around something you might not even want to do in a couple of years? What if you change your mind and you're stuck at a third-rate school because it has the best forensics program?" Shannon says "forensics" as if it means Kiki wants to study toe fungus.

Kiki sighs. "Not every school that isn't an Ivy or in Paris is a third-rate school, for your information, and *yes*, I'm sure. But if I change my mind, I can always transfer. And anyway, how do *you* know you'll always want to study art history? What if *you* decide you don't wanna be a museum curator or gallery owner?"

I watch Shannon and Kiki volley back and forth with fascination. They have nothing in common except that they've both known what they want to do forever, and so they take each other more seriously than anyone else can possibly take either of them. Even watching them clash over it, I know they're playing devil's advocate with each other, making the other one sure she's firm in her choice, because this is just how they do things.

We're a weird crew and we know it: Shannon and her perfect hair and oodles of money, who never misses a party but is still such a mom, into finer things like art and French culture but also totally our group caretaker; Kiki with her mystery obsessions and gothic fashion sense, not to mention total disinterest in dating (despite the rest of us being boy-crazy), who is always the one to remember the little details that matter and gives the most thoughtful gifts as a result; Gia with her narrow interests of Tommy, cheerleading, and making memories, but whose loyalty and focus make her utterly indispensable; and me, who's always up for trying anything and soaking in everybody else, happy to be the guinea pig or test audience for everything from Shannon's glittery eyeliner to Gia's newest choreography.

If we hadn't gone to school together our entire lives and made friends back when we had everything in common because our entire lives were My Little Pony, Dead Man's Float competitions in Kiki's pool, and getting our parents to take us out for ice cream, we might not have anything to do with each other. But we've kept at it and made it work, and now we are a scary and awesome force of mutual support, and I love that about us.

Even in their bitchiest moments, they've never genuinely torn me down for anything. Would that stay true if they knew about Jasmine? Would they look at me differently? *Treat* me differently?

And was Jasmine serious about coming to the Clementine Walker event? I'm not sure I can handle knowing she's in the room if Clementine reads one of her more . . . risqué scenes. Maybe I should bring Chase, share one of my interests with him, given how many football games I've attended. Maybe those scenes will work on him just as well.

Anyway, it's not like Jasmine would've ever touched her books before I recommended them, and she ended up reading four. They're *good*. Maybe Chase will give one a shot. He's not the kind of guy who's, like, "Ew, romance novels are for girls." At least, I don't think he is, though I can't imagine him adding reading on top of schoolwork and football and college applications. It was different with Jasmine. We were free during the summer, and she was already reading at least a book a week, if not more.

It was different with Jasmine, for sure.

Chapter Ten

THEN

"Okay, not that I'm creeping on your reading choices or anything, but I'm pretty sure every single book I've seen you read this summer that wasn't one of my recommendations has been by that woman."

I look up from *Make Me a Catch* to Jasmine standing over my hammock, her long waves swept into a ponytail. It's been three days since we made out, and we haven't talked about it once—we just got up the next morning and proceeded to the next shoot as if nothing had happened, then spent the afternoon at the beach with Keisha, Carter, and the others. I haven't seen her since breakfast this morning. She'd disappeared into her room immediately to do some photo-editing work, and I hadn't expected to see her until dinner. She isn't avoiding me, I don't think, and I'm not avoiding her, but we aren't going out of our way to spend time alone. In fact, this is the first time I've seen her in days without a camera in her hand and a bag of gear in mine.

"She's probably not your thing," I say, embarrassed to be caught devouring so many romance novels. Shannon flashes through my head with her "guilty pleasures is a stupid concept" mantra, and I sit a little straighter. "But she's my favorite romance author. She has a new book coming out in September and I'm rereading everything of hers before it comes out."

"Can I see?" She motions for me to move over in the hammock and I do, aware of every single micro-inch of her bronze skin brushing mine. I hand over the book, refusing to cringe at the hot-pink cover, and she accepts it with a hint of a wicked grin. "Wait, this is a boring scene in an office. Where's the good stuff?"

"You know romance novels have actual plots, right?" I say dryly. "The characters do real things and have brains and stuff?"

"Oh, I'm teasing. But not about the good stuff." She keeps a finger where I left off and flips through the rest until she finds something to her satisfaction. "Ah, here we go.

"'If this is what yardwork does to your body, I need to shake some more leaves from my tree,' said Zoe, sliding a perfectly manicured red fingernail down the line bisecting Drew's pecs and following it with her lips.

"'Baby,' Drew breathed, 'I'll be happy to shake it all for you.' He lifted her in his strong arms and pressed his mouth to hers, inhaling her like the spicy scent of wood smoke on a crisp autumn morning. But his lips weren't content simply to taste her mouth. He rolled her so she was beneath him and left kisses all over her cheeks, her throat, her shoulders, that magnificent collarbone, and the velvety soft pillows of her breasts." Jasmine hands the book back. "You really like that stuff?"

I realize my entire body is clenched tight in reaction to her reading, as if I were trying to stop myself from responding. I relax my limbs, take the book back, and give her an honest answer. "I really do. I'm a sap. I've always been a sap. I never got to grow up seeing my parents sneak kisses or grab each other's butts or whatever it is parents who actually like each other do in movies. Sometimes I think my mom's sad she never had that too, not even for a little bit like your parents. But it's not something everyone who wants it gets, even if they're awesome and put themselves out there. I figure, if I never get it in real life, at least I get it here." I hold up the book. "The way she writes lets you put yourself in her main characters' shoes, because they're not these perfect women; they're messy and not always perfect-looking and they don't all have incredible jobs. They struggle with different shit, but find love anyway. And that's what I want."

I don't look at Jasmine until the words finish rushing out of me, and the teasing smile I expect to see is gone. She's looking at me like . . . I don't know, exactly. But she's taking me seriously and not about to make fun of me for spilling my silly, romantic guts, and I'm grateful.

Her lips do curve again, but there's no real mocking in their tilt. "So, you put yourself in Zoe's non-Louboutins, huh? Do we have to find you a Drew to do yardwork?"

My mind flashes to Chase, who definitely has Drew's defined pecs but I'm pretty sure also has a gardener. I open my mouth to mention him but what comes out instead is, "We're already shaking leaves here." I indicate the trees holding up our hammock. "So."

"Good point. What's next for Zoe, then?"

And because I am half out of my mind, and her low voice reading the excerpt is ringing in my brain, and though we haven't talked about it, I can't get the night of the bonfire out of my head, I say, "Well, you read it." And I drag my decently manicured green nail down to the edge of her tank top and follow it with a kiss.

I spend the longest second in the world waiting for her reaction, gripping the side of hammock in case she rolls out of it with a quickness and I go flying, but finally, she laughs and says, "I did."

And she presses her mouth to mine, inhaling me like the spicy scent of wood smoke on a crisp autumn morning.

NOW

The memory is so clear in my head that I can still hear her voice, and I realize a moment later when a tray slaps down next to Shannon that I am literally hearing her voice. "Hey. What's with the spreadsheet?"

Gia may be a little flighty, but she is a *master* organizer. She turns her laptop to Jasmine so she can see the page with all eight of her chosen colleges listed. "This is where I'm applying," she says, "and here are deadline dates, which schools use the common app, and—well, stuff like that."

She swivels her computer back around, but not before Jasmine catches a glimpse of the last column. "What's DFBC?"

We try really, really hard not to laugh into our food as Gia blushes. "It's, um, Distance from Boston College. That's where Tommy's going. Everyone in his family has gone there for three generations."

Jasmine catches her jaw drop quickly, but I don't miss it, and I'm pretty sure Gia doesn't either. "Oh, that's, uh . . . thorough planning."

"There are a lot of good schools in Boston," Gia says quickly, dragging her fork around her Cobb salad. "It's not like I'd be following him there or anything. I'd be lucky to go to BC, or BU, or Tufts, and Shannon's applying to Harvard and Brown, so she might even be close by."

Clearly, Gia's been practicing her justifications on her parents, who think it's absurd that she wants to go to Boston when she could go to school fifteen minutes away at SUNY Purchase.

My mom says I'm free to go wherever as long as it won't put me in debt for the rest of my life. And since my dad said he'll pay for state school, I've kinda dragged my feet on looking anywhere else. I can't imagine what would be worth taking out loans for if I don't have to. Anyway, I want to major in English, and all schools have English majors, right? So, whatever.

"Where are you applying?" Gia asks her, and I know there's a vague response coming. Jasmine never really wanted to talk about college, said it was too big a decision to leave subject to other people's opinions.

But there's no hesitation when Jasmine says, "I'm

pretty set on NYU, especially since my mom is moving to Jersey. But I've also been thinking about getting off the East Coast entirely, maybe applying somewhere in Colorado or California. Photography's a big hobby of mine and I'm definitely planning to study it more in school, so it'd be cool to get some new surroundings."

I clench my jaw at how readily she just revealed so many personal bits of information, pieces I had to dig halfway to China to get. It's the first time I've heard Jasmine mention her mom since she got to Stratford, and I thought maybe they'd had some sort of falling out, but it sounds like they're as tight as ever.

As annoyed as I am, though, I'm relieved to hear things between Jasmine and her mom are OK and there isn't gonna be as much physical distance as I thought. The weekend we spent with Sylvia Halabi was one of my favorites of the whole summer, and I see why she and Jasmine are so tight. She's cool and effortlessly glamorous, a solid view into what Jasmine will probably look like in thirty years, and an amazing cook. It's hard to picture her with Jasmine's more ruggedly handsome and super Irish dad, but beautiful people always seem to find each other, even if a billion things eventually tear them apart.

"Cool," says Kiki. "NYU's a great school. Lara's applying there too—you guys should talk."

"I'm *thinking* about applying there," I correct her, picking at my turkey burger, and it's true, I am. It's pretty close to home, I can minor in creative writing, and there are plenty of bookstores around so I can hopefully keep working at one, which would offset the tuition difference a little. I've thought about eventually working in publishing and being in the city would be perfect for that. But being at the same school as Jasmine, even if it's enormous? Doesn't sound quite as perfect. "I'm also applying to a few SUNYs, and that's probably where I'll go."

"Where's Chase going?" Gia asks.

I shrug. "Also local, most likely."

Gia's eyes light up—she's such a believer in true love, she's an even sappier romantic than I am—but Shannon looks at me and laughs. "Wait. You're not staying local *because* of him, right? You wouldn't follow a guy to college."

I open my mouth to point out that I've always planned on staying local, but Gia cuts me off. "Just because she's not following him doesn't mean they can't stay together." She turns to me as I'm about to take a bite of my burger. "Do you think you guys will keep dating?"

"It's been a week, G," I say, taking a bite so she won't immediately shoot back with a follow-up question. "What about you?" I ask after I swallow, though I know the answer. It's the surest bet to shifting the conversation. "Do you really think you and Tommy will stay together?"

"I know we will." The look on her face is so simultaneously dreamy and confident, I will Jasmine not to roll her eyes; the rest of us have learned not to.

"That's really nice," Jasmine surprises me by saying, and I look up to see her digging through her salad as if the meaning of life is buried underneath.

Encouraged, Gia launches into the Plan, which means

describing how she and Tommy will stay in the dorms their first year so they can make friends and stuff, but then get an apartment together in between their two schools, provided she gets in somewhere within twenty-five miles of BC. The rest of us have heard this many, many times, but Jasmine nods and says "that makes sense" at all the right points, leaving us free to finish our food and go over our own plans.

I've nearly forgotten Jasmine's there when a familiar voice says, "This seat taken?"

We all look up to see Chase standing there with Lucas Miller, both of their trays piled high with meat and carbs. There's only room for one tray between me and Shannon, and before I can say a word, she smiles at Lucas and says, "I think we can squeeze you in."

"Dude," Chase protests as Lucas slides his tray between ours.

"Gotta be faster than that at the hot chicks' table," Lucas says gleefully, plucking a fry from Kiki's plate even though he has plenty of his own. She snorts but pushes her tray forward slightly. Kiki's not immune to a compliment from a hot guy, even if she doesn't have any interest in dating the ones at our school.

"Tommy doesn't." Chase gestures at where his teammate is strolling up to the table, dropping a kiss on Gia's cheek as he slips in next to her.

"No, Tommy doesn't. My girl saves me a seat because she likes me." Gia rests her head on Tommy's shoulder as he brags. "Maybe you should work on that."

I wish I could physically pull the smug grin off

Tommy's face as he looks from Chase to me. He's only teasing, but I still don't know how to deal with Chase going from fantasy to reality, and I hate him for pointing it out.

"You can have my seat," Jasmine says, getting up and taking her tray with her. "I have a meeting with the college guidance counselor anyway."

"You have a meeting about college guidance you didn't mention even though we were talking about college?" Kiki's meticulously threaded eyebrow shoots up.

"I didn't realize my meeting schedule was of general interest," Jasmine says wryly. "Duly noted for the next meeting of the College Crew."

It's Shannon's turn to snort as Jasmine walks off, but my eyes are on Kiki, even as everyone shifts to make room and Chase's warm body slides in next to mine. Kiki is freakishly smart, but more than that, she's tenacious. If she thinks Jasmine's being shady, no amount of snark is gonna throw her off.

I pray whatever digging she inevitably does into Jasmine leads in a direction that's far, far away from me.

That hope dies in my chest when I see Kiki waiting by my locker at the end of the day. "I know Chase has football practice and Shannon's at French club tonight, so I figured you'd need a ride home."

"Don't you have independent study?" That's what they call having Kiki help produce the school podcast one night a week. It was the best compromise they could come to, given they were desperate to get her on the newspaper and she wouldn't budge.

"Changed to tomorrow night. Alex has a dentist appointment."

How convenient. Thanks, Alex. I hope you don't need a root canal or anything.

"Lucky me," I manage. Ordinarily I'd mean it—Kiki drives a vintage Porsche she and her dad worked on for two years, but it's so small it only comfortably fits one other passenger, so I rarely get to ride in it. But she's up to something. I can see her detective nose twitching.

Sure enough, the questions begin as soon as she pulls out of her spot. "We've barely talked about your summer at the beach," she says, her trademark round-lensed sunglasses obscuring my ability to read her expression. "Did you really only spend your summer tanning and playing assistant to someone at your mom's boss's company?"

Okay, so I stretched the truth a bit. "Yup, pretty much."

"That's it. That was your whole summer."

"Well, you know I started at the Book and Bean a few weeks before school, if that's what you mean." I shade my eyes with my hand and stare out at the neatly manicured lawns of Stratford, house after house in a town with only one apartment complex, which I happen to call home.

She sighs. "Come on, Lar."

"Come on what?" I force myself to face her, and I'll admit, not being able to look her in the eye helps. "What sort of secret mission do you think I was on in freaking North Carolina?"

"I don't know," Kiki says exasperatedly, "but you're

different." She stops at a red light and turns to me. "Look, I'm really happy you finally got with Chase, but are *you* happy for you? Because I thought when this day came, I'd be begging you to stop mentioning his name every three seconds and asking us what to wear on dates and how soon is too soon to get naked."

At that, I laugh. "So . . . you're bothered that I'm not as annoying as you thought I'd be?"

"It's more than that. You stood up to Shannon about sharing your shit with Jasmine. And since the summer, you . . . walk taller, or something. Chase obviously sees something different in you, and I'm just saying, I see it too."

Okay, this was *definitely* not the conversation I expected. I've always wondered if maybe Kiki lived somewhere under the rainbow, given her total disinterest in the guys at Stratford, but I kinda figured she was too sophisticated for them. She's the type to, like, sleep with her brilliant professor in college. But maybe—

"That sounded like I was hitting on you. I'm not hitting on you," she clarifies. "I just feel like I'm missing out on something big in your life and it's kind of killing me. Not because I'm a nosy piece of shit but because you're one of my best friends."

For a moment, I feel a twinge of disappointment. Not that I wanted Kiki to hit on me—there's enough confusion in my head as it is—but I'd kill to be able to talk to another girl who's kissed a girl, who's . . . been with a girl. I want to ask her what the fuck it means and how I know if it *does* mean something.

But, I realize, Kiki's giving me an opening for

something else. And it's not everything, but it's not nothing. "It's not something big," I say, feeling shy and silly, and grateful when the light turns green and she has to tear her eyes away from me. "But I kind of loved the work I did this summer. The person I assisted? She was amazing. She did all this photography and web stuff, and I feel like I learned that there are more things to do with your life than, like, doctor or lawyer or accountant or whatever else every kid from here does. I don't know, it just got me feeling . . . open. And optimistic. Excited for the future and trying new things. Not that I have any photography talent, but . . . writing, maybe?" I can't believe I just told Kiki that. I can't believe I'm still talking. I can't believe I am about to tell her my second biggest secret. "I've been writing. A book. A romance, actually."

"Lara! That's awesome!" Her smile is so big and genuine, and it makes me smile too. "I had no idea you were interested in writing. I didn't know *what* you were interested in, really, other than Chase."

The comment stings, but it also makes me laugh. "Surprise! And no, it isn't Chase-and-Lara fanfiction, I swear."

"Thank *God*. That's really, really cool. I can't believe I didn't know you were into writing before, but it totally makes sense."

"Yeah?"

"Yeah! You've always liked reading for fun, and you're always the first to want to learn or try something new, which probably makes great research. Don't think I've forgotten how many times you've let me fingerprint you."

I snort. "I couldn't if I wanted to. That ink stained my fingers for, like, a week."

"And I appreciate it!" She grins. "But okay, so, not to get all Gia on you, but don't tell me there was *zero* romance this summer. *Something* cooled your Chase panties all the way down."

I groan. "Do you have to phrase everything so extremely gross?"

"Yes."

"There might have been . . . some kissing," I allow. "But that's all I'll say about that. And let the record show that my Chase panties are still firmly on. Are we done now?"

"We're done," she agrees, pulling up to my building. "But Lar, I'm really, really glad you told me. And if you ever wanna use those newfound web skills, I wouldn't mind having help making some pretty ads for *Kiki on the Case*. Paid, of course."

I tap my finger to my chin. "I don't know if you could afford me, but we'll talk." Impulsively, I lean over and press a kiss to the top of her head. "Thanks, Keeks." I jump out of the car before she can yell at me for showing emotion.

But there's no yelling. "Lar?"

I turn back. "Yeah?"

"Whoever you were kissing . . . I think they must've been really good for you."

My mind lingers on her use of "they" long after she leaves me standing in the Porsche's dust.

Chapter Eleven

The thing about using your cell phone as your alarm clock is it's hard to avoid seeing your notifications first thing when you wake up. The minute I open my eyes, I see a new episode of *Kiki on the Case* has been released.

Oh, and the title of the episode is "Secret Relationships in History."

It's too early to deal with my stress over whether or not she's trying to send me a message, or worse, if there's something pointed at me *in* it, so I skip my usual routine of scrolling through everyone's posts and pictures to wake myself up and instead hop straight into the shower.

I try to think about literally anything else as the hot spray rains, but everything from Homecoming to Chase to college feels charged. I went to sleep around eleven last night, and there hadn't been a new episode then; what was so important Kiki had to post it first thing this morning? Not to mention the time she must've taken to edit it. Did she even sleep?

I guess I should be grateful I got to, thanks to having no idea this was coming.

Sighing in defeat, I finish my shower quickly and throw some mousse in my natural waves rather than going through the whole curling routine that's been keeping me extra cute since Jasmine introduced me to it. I don't feel like looking extra cute; I want to blend so deeply into the woodwork even Kiki and her eagle eyes won't see me. The dress I had picked out for today gets pushed aside in favor of a long-sleeved T-shirt and jeans, and I skip makeup entirely.

Chase will probably walk right through me.

Today, that's all I want.

As usual, Shannon's right on time to pick me up, and Gia's in the back seat, but no sign of Kiki, who's usually picked up first. "Keeks is taking the Porsche in again today," Shannon explains as I climb into the front seat of her 4Runner, "but don't worry." She taps her dashboard. "It's basically like she's here."

Shannon is playing the newest episode of *Kiki on the Case,* because of course she is.

"I haven't listened yet," I say cautiously. "What'd I miss?"

"She's putting secret couples from history on blast. Did you know Eleanor Roosevelt was a lesbian? She had a secret lover and everything."

The coffee my mom handed me this morning sloshes in my stomach. "You don't say."

I have to warn Jasmine today about the conversations that are gonna be floating around, and about the very distinct possibility that Kiki has somehow pieced together the truth about us. Thinking about any and all of it makes me wanna die.

For a moment, I'm worried I spoke aloud, because suddenly Shannon's car is turning onto Jasmine's street.

"What are we doing here?" Gia asks, and I'm relieved I don't have to.

"Jasmine's car is in the shop, so I told her we'd give her a ride."

That Shannon knows her car is in the shop, and that Shannon is who Jasmine went to for help, punches me in the gut. They're *really* becoming friends, and I don't know whether the idea of not being Shannon's number one anymore or the idea of not being Jasmine's number one at Stratford bothers me more. How did they bond like this? When? Where was I?

Gia huffs the tiniest bit. Everyone knows that in our close-knit group of four, Shannon and I are the tightest; when my mom was still finding her footing in the job market and working later hours than Child Protective Services would've found acceptable, the Salter mansion's open-door policy was a lifesaver, rendering us inseparable. But that doesn't mean any one of us are gonna be cool with a fifth wheel.

Shannon pretends not to notice.

The sound of a door slamming makes us all look up. As if Jasmine knew I was gonna be wearing my blandest outfit, she's wearing what must be one of her loudest—black-and-white-checkered hip huggers, a cropped hot-pink sweater that looks gorgeous with her deeply tanned skin, and big gold hoops that poke through her thick, silky curtain of hair. She's usually a few inches taller than me, but today she's wearing platforms that lift her a few extra.

She looks like she wants to be noticed.

I try not to think about whom she'd like to be noticed *by*.

It's a few weeks into the school year and I haven't heard any rumors of Jasmine getting with anyone or even flirting, though I've heard of plenty of guys expressing interest. She's getting a reputation as mysterious and elusive—everything I thought she was before I got to know her. Everything she's been to me again since she moved here.

This summer she felt like someone I'd been born to know, and now I feel like I can't predict a damn thing.

Which I guess is back to being how she likes it.

"Good morning!" Shannon greets her sunnily as she slips in the backseat with Gia, and Jasmine grunts in the universal language of "I haven't had my coffee yet." Shannon laughs and says that clearly a stop at the Starbucks drive-thru will be required.

Jasmine mumbles her appreciation. Even fully decked out, she has never been a morning person, though she does warm up a bit when Gia declares her outfit cute.

We're driving for about a minute when Jasmine speaks up. "What are you guys listening to? Is that Kiki?"

I cringe as Gia launches into an explanation of the episode, glad that Jasmine can't see me from her seat behind me.

"Secret relationships. Interesting." Jasmine sure sounds awake now. "So . . . fraught. I wonder what brought that on."

I dig my nails into the seat, not caring if it chips the pink polish I applied last night.

"It must suck to have to keep a relationship secret," Gia muses. "I mean, I guess it's kind of romantic, having something just between the two of you, but if I couldn't hold Tommy's hand in the hallway or kiss him at the movies—"

"And in the lunch room, and in class, and at parties, and at—"

"Oh, shut up," Gia says to Shannon as Jasmine snorts and I full-on laugh. Gia likes to think she's restrained about PDA, but she's delusional. She would be a terrible spy.

Definitely not a candidate for a secret relationship.

I try to imagine Gia in my shoes, fooling around with a girl under blankets on the couch or under the cover of starlight, and I can't. It had felt then like it could happen to anyone, like female friends who were comfortable with each other could fall onto each other's mouths and it was all cool. But would that have happened if it'd been Gia on the beach—Gia, who was obsessed with Tommy's masculine forearms and deep voice and the earthy smell of his cologne? Shannon, maybe, if she thought it somehow made her worldly. Shannon would probably shout about it from the rooftops.

And suddenly, it hits me. I'm here drowning in self-reflection while Shannon and Jasmine get closer. Shannon may be flirting with Lucas, but they aren't a Thing, not yet. And Shannon's been known to surprise with her dating choices, especially if she thinks landing them is a fun challenge. Is *that* what's going on here? Is Jasmine dressed up because Shannon's picking her up? Is Shannon picking her up like people pick up people they're dating?

The wave of pain that hits is fast and furious, and I don't even realize it's coming until I've already moaned out loud, forcing Shannon to stop short. "Jesus, Lara. Are you OK?"

I don't know, I want to say. *Tell me you're not hooking up with Jasmine and maybe I will be.*

I don't know why that's the thought that comes to my head. I don't know why this hurts. I don't know what I feel like I'm losing because I don't know *what* I'm losing. All I know is the thought of them together—like, *really* together—feels like a stab wound to the chest.

"Fine, sorry," I croak, and Shannon makes a teasing comment about me being a drama queen. Which . . . is maybe exactly what I *am* being. And anyway, I have *Chase.* I am dating Chase fucking Harding. I don't know how serious we are or will be but I do know what he listens to in the car and what lines make him laugh at movies and what his mouth tastes like, and that is plenty. So, what am I getting hung up about?

There's the lightest squeeze on my shoulder, so gentle I'd think I was imagining it if it weren't for the searing warmth coming through my baggy shirt. And like that, my question is answered: the knowing when I need a touch, when I need to be remembered, when I need affection. That quiet, intuitive kindness. That's what I'm getting hung up about.

I lift my hand to squeeze hers back, but it's already gone.

Chapter Twelve

After a week full of weirdness, I manage to pull myself out of it in time for Chase's game Friday night and our subsequent date. Granted, it takes some pushing from Shannon to get me fully decked out in fangirl paint, from Chase's number 14 boldly drawn on my face in blue to "Go Chase" scrawled down my arms. But I look pretty cute with it, and judging by the way Chase's face lights up when he sees me, he agrees.

Next to me, Shannon's forgone face paint in favor of a pro-Lucas sign, and she keeps whacking me in the face, but I don't care. Chase is having one of the best games I've ever seen, and we spend a decent portion of the evening on our feet, cheering as he completes pass after pass, his arm finding its targets with terrifying accuracy.

On any given day, he's good, but this is next-level. If there's a scout hiding somewhere at this game, Chase is getting a scholarship for sure.

"He's so fucking hot," the girl in front of us whispers

to her friend as Chase accepts a high five from Lucas after rushing the ball halfway down the field before getting slammed to the ground, and I feel my cheeks heat with pride. The Stratford rumor mill definitely hasn't missed that there's something between us, even if there's only been one real date. He may not be mine in the way Tommy is Gia's, but it's enough for me to get the feeling that comes with knowing pretty much every girl in the room would kill to be you.

"Larissa Bogdan is such a lucky bitch," the friend whispers back as if to prove my point, and I nearly break my nasal passages holding back a snort.

Shannon is unconcerned with being discreet. "He's the lucky one, actually," she leans forward and says, "and I'm the only one who gets to call her a bitch."

The girls, who can't be older than sophomores, look like they're gonna pee in their tight jeans when they turn around and see us there. I can tell the girl who called me a lucky bitch wants to say she's sorry, but she's having trouble getting words out.

I elbow Shannon in the side and she laughs. "I *am* lucky," I say before the girl can cry or whatever. "He's great, isn't he?"

Two jerky puppet nods in response, and then there's a roar from the crowd and we look up to see Chase has thrown for another touchdown. "That's number three for the Saints!" brings us all to our feet. "Chase Harding is on fire tonight!"

Chase catches my eye and bows, and I'm gonna melt into the floor, if the girls in front of me don't kill me first. But I remain cool and blow a kiss back.

"Aren't you glad you listened to me about the face paint?" Shannon coos, pushing an unruly blond curl behind my ear. "Look how much he loves having his own personal cheerleader."

The description makes me bristle, but I can't argue with how it *was* her idea to sport the paint, and he *does* seem to like it. "Pretty sure it's my legs in this outfit he loves," I say anyway, and Shannon sticks out her tongue.

We continue to tease each other and cheer and wave at Gia during her routines and send annoying updates to Kiki, who couldn't care less about the game and is home glued to some true crime documentary. Mostly, I observe Chase—the agility with which he weaves between players, the way the sweat glows on his forearms, the strength in his legs. I've spent years watching every line of his body move on this field, but tonight is different. Tonight, I don't have to pretend I'm eyeing all the guys equally. I don't have to pretend I could just as happily be anywhere else. I can stare at him and howl his name and whistle in his direction and do all the things I've always done in my head, loud and proud and with his number right on my face.

So I do. I'm Chase's number one cheerleader. Next to me, Shannon is the same for Lucas, though he's only joined Chase at our table once this week and they don't have any plans this weekend. It's enough to make me wonder how significant her interest is in him, and whether that means that anything going on between her and Jasmine is all in my head.

Not that it matters.

I'm here with Chase. Who's a complete and total rock star and who I'm pretty sure just smiled at me again.

I stay completely glued to the field for the final quarter, and even Shannon gives up trying to make Lucas happen and joins me and everyone else in cheering on Chase, who's dangerously close to breaking the school's record for passing yards in single game. There's no question which team is going to win, but I'm biting my nails as I watch his stats edge up. Every time he completes another pass, there's another roar and another announcement of his yardage total.

Looking at him, you might think he's completely chill about it from his enthusiastic high fives and "whatever, man" shrugs, but I see the way his shoulders tense with each call. How his smiles are forced. I *know* Chase. Getting mixed up with Jasmine may have made me forget for a minute, but he's been here since well before I knew she existed. I know him, and—

The crowd goes absolutely nuts, and even though my eyes are on the field, my own head clearly made me miss something. It isn't until Shannon grabs my wrists and screams "He did it!" that I realize Chase passed for another twenty yards, officially taking him over the 463 he needed to wipe the last guy from the record books. I scream right along with her, doing a little cheer from my seat I remember from my freshman year stint on the JV squad. Chase yanks off his helmet, looks up at me, and laughs. I blow him a kiss and he catches it and smashes it right against his mouth, and suddenly the cheers turn to whistling and laughter and I realize we have an audience. Heat rises into my cheeks but honestly, I'm way more overwhelmed with pride than shame.

Coach Robinson calls the team back to attention to finish out the game, and the rest of us fidget in our seats as they run out the clock with benchwarmers (though they keep Chase on to see how high he can go) until we can celebrate properly.

Finally, the buzzer sounds, and the stands explode. I hug Shannon and even the girls in front of me, all while keeping an eye on Chase accepting one-armed hugs and high fives from everyone on the field. It's hard to be pissed about a loss when a guy literally set a record defeating you, I guess.

There's never been a less shocking announcement than the one in which Chase is named MVP, and I clap with pride as he's awarded the trophy that changes hands from game to game in Stratford tradition. He poses for a couple of pictures, then takes the mic for the usual speech about how everyone played a great game, blah blah blah.

"This was such an amazing night," he says after the standard opener, "and there's one person who made it all the more special by being here." He gestures at the stands, and there's a quick flash of envy in my brain before I realize his hand is extended toward *me*. "Look at my girl, up there with my number on her gorgeous face and my name on her arm. How can any guy *not* pass for four hundred ninety-six yards when he's got her on his side?"

I can't decide if I'm elated or mortified, but at least my head being in a fog makes it easy to ignore the pain of Shannon's nails digging crescent-shaped valleys into each of my arms. I'm pretty sure they're drawing blood.

"I was gonna wait until later to ask you, but I'm feeling so good, I can't wait—Larissa Bogdan, will you go to Homecoming with me?"

Everyone's eyes are on me as if they were stuck to my painted skin. But the truth is, I'm not shy, and I've known since I was twelve what the answer to this question is, even if it took him way too long to ask it.

I wish people would just admit what they want when they want it, I hear Jasmine's voice rasp in my brain, and without hesitation I yell back "Hell yeah, I will!"

For the millionth time that night, the crowd goes wild.

"I hope I didn't embarrass you," he says as we walk to his car, his arm wrapped around my waist. It's a short walk, since he has the spot closest to the school on game nights, but it's long enough for me to take a good look at his smile and realize that's only partly true. He likes the idea of making me blush. I wonder if he would've preferred if I'd responded shyly instead of in an outburst. But he doesn't exactly look disappointed either.

He looks . . . like he is really, really into me.

"You didn't," I assure him, and I'm pretty sure it's true. "I'm excited to go to Homecoming with you. I was hoping you'd ask tonight."

"Even before I had the game of my life?"

I laugh. "Did you think you needed to in order to convince me to go with you?"

"No, but I figured it couldn't hurt," he says with a grin. We get to his car and he presses me against it and leans down to kiss me, his mouth sweet with the taste of Gatorade.

Whistles and catcalls sound around us as we make out against his car, exactly as I've always pictured, and it's weird and amazing and confusing to have it all come to life. But even the handle pressed against my back has figured into my daydreams, and it's prepped me for the discomfort.

I want to feel everything.

Chase does not quite share that desire. "I'm sorry," he says, pulling away, "but this is killing my neck. You kinda take 'shorty' to a whole new level."

"Hey, I'm a full five feet, thank you very much."

"And you are a very cute five feet," he says, wrapping me in a hug and lifting me off my toes for another quick kiss. "But I am a much less cute six-three and I've spent my entire night getting completely wrecked. I think my body's at its limit for stretching in unnatural directions." He waggles his eyebrows. "At least for another ten minutes or so."

"Subtle. Do you want me to drive?"

"Nah, by the time you adjust the seat to your height the party will probably be over." I whack him on the arm, and he laughs. "Come on—faster we get there, faster we find a more comfortable place to get back to what we were doing."

I open my mouth to point out we can always skip the party, but we really can't. Chase is the star of the night, and at some point, Hunter Ferris's makeup party for the one Jasmine snatched away has definitely turned into a party in his honor. No one would forgive me if he didn't show. I'll probably have to get used to this—all the stuff that comes with being a star player's girlfriend—and while it used to seem cool in my head, now it makes me feel . . . impatient. Exhausted.

Inevitably, my mind wanders.

THEN

I'm quickly running out of outfits to wear to parties in the Outer Banks, hoping people won't notice how frequently I'm wearing the same shorts or jeans with different tank tops from the sales rack at Urban Outfitters. Jasmine sports something I've never seen every single night—sequined dresses or brightly colored capris or pleather leggings she wears as comfortably as a second skin. Even after getting closer, or maybe because of it, I haven't had the nerve to ask her to borrow anything.

There *is* a dress I haven't worn yet—it's a gorgeous turquoise with cool beaded embroidery winding down from the single strap—that I packed in case my mom made me go to something fancy as her date. I've been saving it for a special occasion, though I have no idea what occasion that might be. Almost everything we go to is messy with sand and beer and ash, and we come away reeking of smoke and weed that I keep promising my mom is not the result of my own consumption.

Suddenly, the thought of doing it all over again tonight is exhausting. It's just another house party at

Carter's, but it means straightening my hair, and doing my makeup, and making small talk with whatever tourists he's picked up on the beach, and nursing a beer I don't even like, and dodging smokers, and politely rejecting come-ons that I don't want, and I just . . . don't feel like it. I spend most of the parties only hanging out with Jasmine anyway, playing at mixing drinks, or talking about books, or prying for details of her life at home, where she takes pictures for the school paper and goes to rock shows after having Shabbat dinner with her mom most Friday nights, and I can do that here.

The image of a lazy night on the couch, watching movies, sharing a blanket, skin grazing skin . . . I shake my head to dislodge it. That's not how this goes. That's not what this is. She'll want to go to Carter's party, because in real life, she wants Carter. I don't know how many times they might've hooked up since that first night, but I couldn't forget Keisha's "like bunnies" if I tried. They—

"Hey, any chance you wanna skip this thing tonight and stay here?"

I whirl around to see Jasmine standing in the doorway to my room, her hair in her usual party waves but her face makeup-free, her body clad in nothing but a tank top and pajama shorts, her legs glittering lightly with sparkly lotion that I happen to know smells like peaches.

"Movie night?" I offer, hoping she can't tell how excited I am that we're on the same page.

"I'll go make popcorn."

Our parents are out at a dinner tonight, which they are so often that I would think it was a cover if I hadn't heard my mother firmly confirm reservations while curling her hair and touching up her lipstick all at the same time. She can be an octopus of multitasking when she needs to. It's what makes her so good at her job, and also a little frightening. We haven't spent as much time together this summer as I'd imagined when she floated the change of plans by me, but we promised tomorrow we'd have a Saturday brunch, just the two of us, and I'm strangely looking forward to it.

I slide on some tinted lip balm and put my hair, still wet from the shower, in two simple braids. It's a relief to slip into a T-shirt and shorts instead of a party outfit, but I have to shake the momentary urge to put on something nice to impress Jasmine.

"Your hair looks cute like that," she says when I walk into the living room, where she's splayed out on the couch, her tank top riding up an inch.

Warmth tinges my cheeks at her compliment. "Thanks. I didn't know what else to do with it. Didn't feel like blow-drying it." I fiddle with the wet ends. "Don't you dare give me an 'I told you so,' but I've been thinking about what you said in the gardens. About making a change. Maybe."

She bites her lip to keep from laughing, and I stick out my tongue. "It was only a suggestion!" she calls over her shoulder as the microwave beeps and she hops up to get the puffed-up bag of popcorn. "But I would be totally pro a curly bob. Not super short or anything, but like, curls down to here." She indicates her throat just past her chin. "Your hair's naturally wavy anyway, right? It'd be so much less work."

"That sounds ... kind of cute, actually," I say, but what I'm thinking is whether Shannon would think I could pull it off, and if Chase prefers long hair. His dating history would suggest he does. "I was also thinking of maybe going lighter. Like, actual blond—not my something-in-between-blond-and-brown color."

She tips her head, examining me in a way that makes me feel warm all over, and nods. "You would look so good blond, I bet." She puts the popcorn on the counter, walks over, and delicately lifts a braid. "Yeah, I totally see it."

I forget how to breathe until the braid once again grazes my shoulder. "You think?"

"I definitely think. There's a cool wig shop I've been wanting to check out, for fun and maybe a few pictures. We could try it, see what you think. If you like it, I know a great place only a few miles away with a stylist named Valentina who's a *genius*. She used to style my mom's hair when we came here before my parents' divorce, and trust me, my mother would not let anyone who couldn't medal in the hair Olympics touch her precious locks."

It sounds scary and fun, and I'm not sure which emotion is winning. I haven't changed my look in ... ever, really. The one I have now has always worked well enough—it's friend-approved, mom-adored, and even if I haven't gotten the Boy, it certainly looks good enough to get *other* boys for some fun here and there.

What would they all think if I came back with such a drastic change?

No, wait, screw that—what would *I* think?

"Let's try it," I say before I can let anyone else's voice

make me second-guess myself. "It's just temporary, right? No commitment until I see if I like it."

"Exactly. No cutting or dyeing until you get to see it on you. But I bet you're gonna look amazing. I have an eye for these things."

Considering how good Jasmine looks on a daily basis, I don't doubt it. Not that I say that. "What do you want to watch?" I ask instead.

"Something fun and glamorous." She grabs some peanut M&Ms from their constant spot in the kitchen cabinet and shakes them into the popcorn, then brings the bowl to the couch and pats the seat next to her. "I can always watch *Ocean's 8* or *Crazy Rich Asians* or whatever for the zillionth time, or we can try something else if you're in the mood."

Those words aren't meant to be suggestive, but my skin prickles anyway. Her tank top is hanging low and her hair looks soft to the touch and we haven't established any sorts of rules, but it feels like I would be breaking one if I told her I was, in fact, very in the mood.

"Whatever you want," I croak as I join her, careful not to let my skin brush hers. She shrugs and puts on *Crazy Rich Asians*, which she's already watched at least twice this summer. It *is* a fun movie, but it's not a particularly sexy one, and I hope that watching it like a hawk will get these ridiculous thoughts out of my brain. But then she stretches the gold chenille throw blanket over my lap and I get the scent of her peach lotion and even Henry Golding can't bring me back from the brink of madness.

Jasmine, of course, doesn't notice a thing. She's glued

to the screen, commenting on how much she loves every single character's wardrobe and jewelry, oblivious to how badly I want to lean over and kiss her bare shoulder that's inches away. I'm too foggy-brained to even think about how weird it is that *I* want to. The couple of times we've made out have somehow felt like the simplest, most obvious moves, but in reality, they're so much more complicated.

But what I want right now isn't complicated. What I want is very, very simple.

I wish people would just admit what they want when they want it.

Before I know what I'm doing, I'm resting my chin on her shoulder. Leaving the lightest of kisses behind on her skin. Glancing at her for a reaction.

Her eyelids flutter shut.

Okay then.

I kiss her smooth shoulder very deliberately this time. Again, a trace of my tongue. Again, a nip of my teeth. She inhales sharply, stops reaching for popcorn, stops saying a word about jeweled rings and couture dresses. I push her hair to the side and kiss my way to the top of her spine, bracing myself on her bare thigh. And then her hand covers mine, helps it slide over her skin, no doubt leaving peach-scented traces on my palm. It's so much. Everything smells and tastes and feels so good and it's making me dizzy.

I move in closer, my breasts brushing her back, and we fall on our sides on the couch, me still kissing her shoulder, her throat while she slides my hand higher, over her cotton shorts, up to her smooth, flat belly. My fingers have the easiest access to her waistband, but her grip isn't as strong, her desires less pointed and clear, and I'm not sure how far to go or how far I *want* to go. I settle for grazing my fingertips over the front of her shorts. She must be as wired as I am because it seems like enough.

It's growing unbearably hot under the blanket, but one rule neither of us says aloud is that it can't come off. As long as there's a blanket, as long as there isn't anything out in the open, it's easy to imagine there's nothing at all. And we need to imagine there's nothing at all, because if this is something—if the fact that I desperately want to slide my hand down her shorts is real—then what are we?

What am I?

It's one summer.

You can't change into a different person over a summer.

Chapter Thirteen

THEN

Maybe you can't become a different person in one summer, but you can definitely look like one. I can't stop
checking myself out in the mirror with this wig on.
"Holy cow."

"I knew that was the one." Jasmine comes up behind me, momentarily pulling my gaze away from myself with her flame-blue blunt-cut bangs. "That color is
perfect."

It is. It's strange because it isn't mine, but it *feels* like
me. Even in this short, curly wig, this is a look I could
get used to, a look I'd love to keep seeing in the mirror.
But it's a big change, and my palms keep itching to send
a selfie to my friends for their approval.

Instead, I change the subject. "Have you ever colored
your hair?"

"Nah, not for real." She takes off her wig and replaces

it with a shaggy lavender one. "My friend Laila—the only other Syrian at my school—used to love putting chalk in our hair before shows, but our moms would've killed us if we did more than that." She affects a melodious, lightly accented tone that's even lower than hers. "Y'haram, Jasmine! What did you do to your beautiful hair?! Steta would be rolling in her grave!"

"I thought your mom was super into fashion."

"She is, but pastel hair isn't exactly her idea of it. My mom is Gucci and Chanel, not Manic Panic. Her idea of letting loose is wearing sunglasses with blue-tinted lenses. She's very classic. All earth tones and whatnot."

"Hmm, I can see that with your dad."

Jasmine snorts. "She dresses classy, but she's the loudest human you will ever meet. My dad used to wear literal earplugs when her family was visiting. Honestly, I can't believe they lasted six years."

"You weren't exactly shocked by the divorce, huh?" I tug on the wig's curls a little to see how it'd look a tiny bit longer, but it ruins the effect.

"Not at all. They fought about evvvverything. And my mom's parents hated that she married a gentile while my dad's parents hated that he married a Jew, and it was not great. My mom kept the house, my dad moved his business up to the city and got that huge-ass house in Stratford while keeping this one for the summer, and by the time my bat mitzvah hit I had nothing left to ask for because I was already spoiled to death."

"That explains so much."

She grins. "Doesn't it? How about you? What's your single mom story?"

"Not much of a story," I say with a shrug. "My mom was waiting tables to put herself through college. My dad picked her up. A few dates later, I happened. My mom wanted to keep me, my dad didn't, and they compromised on him paying child support and otherwise disappearing. Ta-da! You have the beautiful, well-adjusted teenager you see before you today."

"You *are* pretty well-adjusted for someone who knows her dad didn't want her to exist."

I smile into the mirror, poking dimples into my cheeks. I learned a long time ago that it was entirely his loss, and my mom is enough awesome for three parents. "Why yes, I suppose I am."

"I could never."

"Please. She who laughs in the face of divorce." I turn to face Jasmine, who's pulled the wig from her head and is slumped against the wall, letting the lavender strands dangle. "Hey, are you okay?"

"I'm fine." A slight, forced smile drifts across her face as quickly as the ocean breeze. "But are you? For real? Because yeah, maybe I was cool with them getting divorced, but not so much with my dad moving to New York and dropping me to only Christmases and summers."

The shop is empty except for us, and the older woman behind the counter is sitting with her feet up and a small TV turned on to soap operas, so I imagine she won't mind if we make ourselves comfortable. I drop onto the floor across from Jasmine and take the wig from her hands before she can twist off all the artificial hair with her anxious fingers.

"I am," I say, and I mean it. "My mom has had to be double the parent, but she's amazing, and I couldn't ask for better. Is that why you never talk about home and your school friends? I'd never even heard of Laila before today."

She shrugs and slides down the wall onto the linoleum. "I guess. It just feels like two different worlds—there and here. It's like it isn't even part of the same life."

For a second, my mind flashes to when we were feeling each other up under the watchful eyes of Constance Wu and Gemma Chan, and I know exactly what she means.

"What are Laila and your other friends doing this summer? I'm surprised you don't have any other school friends here."

"Asheville's pretty kick-ass during the summer, so most people stay home and go hiking and to festivals and whatever. Laila and our friend Kendall work at a day camp together. I get to come back at the end of every summer and listen to two months of private jokes before everything gets back to normal."

I pull off my blond curls and toss the wig to her. "You can't win, huh?"

She spins the wig on her finger and exhales into a self-deprecating laugh. "God, I sound like such a brat. Boo-fucking-hoo that I spend the summers in a gorgeous, expensive beach house with a pool and hot tub."

"You get to boo-fucking-hoo that you're lonely, Jas," I say softly, because I realize that's exactly what she is. Her friends at home feel conditional, her friends here feel like surface-level entertainment, she isn't with the parent she knows wants to spend time with her, and she *is* with the one she feels doesn't give a shit.

She is lonely and hurting and has been for a long time.

A tear forms in one of her eyes and is wiped away so quickly I almost think I've imagined it. "Hashtag onlychildproblems. And hey," she says, tossing the wig back, "I'm not lonely this summer, right?"

I smile. "Sure as hell not."

"So, are you doing it?" She nods toward the hair. "It looked damn good."

Jasmine thinking it looks damn good shouldn't have any effect on me, but the heat crawling up my skin would suggest it does. Still, I force myself to shake it and think about what *I* want.

And I thought it looked pretty damn good too.

I never do this. I'm the opposite of lonely; pretty much every decision in my life involves a consultation with my mom, or Shannon, or both. This would be me, and only me, making a choice, alongside someone who isn't gonna be there on the first day of school when people see it for the first time.

Me.

"Yeah," I say, getting to my feet and holding out a hand to Jasmine. "I'm doing it."

She takes my hand and grins as I pull her up. "Good. Because I already made the appointment, and it's in fifteen minutes."

"Jasmine!"

"It takes time to get an opening there!" she says,

holding up her hands in the universal gesture of inno-
cence. "I wasn't gonna make you go if you didn't want to."

"Hmph." I turn back to the mirror and put the wig on
one last time, just to make sure.

I look really freaking good.

"Fine," I say, taking it off and putting it back on the
mannequin while Jasmine puts back the wigs she'd
been sporting. "Let's go change my life or whatever."

Chapter Fourteen

NOW

It takes forever to get through the swarm of congratulatory partiers once we arrive at Ferris's. Everyone wants a piece of Chase—a picture, an autograph, a hug, a kiss on the cheek. . . . I can't imagine what else they'd be looking for if he were single, but he made very clear at the game that he isn't, and I walk through the crowd feeling like I'm wearing a full-body halo.

"Sorry it's such a circus," he murmurs to me when yet another guy comes over and claps a meaty hand on his shoulder. It seems like every athlete at Stratford has come out for this, whether they're into football or not. News travels fast. I had to set my phone to Do Not Disturb because it was lighting up with notifications from every single social media app. People aren't just cheering on the team's win or Chase's record; they're sharing videos of him asking me to the dance, of me responding, of their heart-eye emojis and dreams of finding a guy like that.

It's not like I'm unused to getting some attention, but this is seriously next-level. Even Shannon's completely out-of-control sweet sixteen didn't storm social media like this, and she had performers from Cirque du Soleil.

I can't see Shannon, but I can hear her across the room, laughing and flirting and, from the sound of it, getting deep into Ferris's extensive liquor stash. I wonder if she's with Gia and Tommy, or with Lucas, or with someone else entirely. I'm just glad she's *here*. It means she's not sulking over not being the star of the night, like she did last year when Tommy's promposal to Gia way overshadowed hers, or when dating-my-lab-partner-Jamie Taylor dyed their hair to match the nonbinary flag the same day Shannon got her first lowlights.

"Well, if it isn't the king and queen of the evening!" Linus Doyle swoops forward with an exaggerated bow, Hunter Ferris himself at his heels.

"We have reservedeth a room for the royal couple," Ferris says in a regal voice, "but do not breaketh any shit, for it is my parents' room. Eth."

"Dude, why would you let us use your parents' room?" Chase asks, and I like him even more for it.

Ferris shrugs. "They're out of town for the week, and the maid's coming tomorrow anyway," he answers in his regular voice. "Just don't be gross and don't try on any of my dad's cravats."

"Why would—"

"I know, you wouldn't think people would have to be

told that," Ferris says, cutting me off and glaring at Linus, "and yet."

Chase twines his fingers in mine and gives my hand a little tug. "You wanna?"

I think back to watching him dominate the field, to the smiles and winks he threw my way, the proud thanks at the end. I think of all the times I've admired his body in uniform or at pool parties or just walking down the hall wearing jeans way too well. I think of how the last time I took off my clothes with someone, it was my last night in the Outer Banks, a single night that felt much too honest at the time yet has been anything but since the first day of school.

And I say, "Yeah, I wanna."

Ferris wasn't kidding when he said they saved us a room; there's a sign with a crown bearing a number 14 on the door and a little bowl next to the bed with more condoms than anyone could possibly use over the length of a party. My stomach flips at the sight. I've done my share of fooling around, but none of it has actually necessitated one of those colorful little packets.

Not that I'm opposed, and especially not with Chase; he's been the guy I've imagined my first time with for years. Though maybe not in some guy's parents' bed at a house party, before we've gone on a second real date.

Chase laughs when he sees them. "I see someone was a little optimistic." He closes the door behind us and swoops down to drop a kiss on my cheek. "Don't worry. I have zero expectation of using those tonight."

"Good," I say without thinking, and before I can wonder if that was a mistake, Chase lifts me in his arms and kisses me.

"I thought your muscles hurt," I mumble against his lips.

"Oh, right," he says, and he drops me on the bed with a wicked grin.

"Hey!" But there's no time for my teasing protest because he's crawling up the bed and taking my face in his hands—paint smears be damned—and we're making out like everyone else in the house, in the world, has disappeared.

"I hope this paint comes off in the wash," I murmur as Chase kisses my neck, my arms definitely staining the linen.

"I hope it doesn't," he says, pushing aside the shoulder of my shirt to kiss the skin it was hiding. "There should be evidence of Stratford's newest record holder scoring yet again that same night."

"That's awful."

"I'm just teasing." His fingers creep up my shirt, grazing over my belly button ring, waiting to see if they'll be stopped on their journey to my special occasion lace bra.

They won't.

I can feel the exact moment he realizes it.

"Hi there," I say, and he laughs into my neck.

I help him slip my shirt off and then there's no more talking, no more teasing, no more laughing. The kissing is fast and furious, hands wandering, and his shirt joins mine, casually tossed on the floor. We're skin-on-lace and skin-on-skin and it's all good until we start hearing catcalls through the door.

"Get it, Harding!"

"Go, boy, go!"

Oh God. I want to die, but Chase wrenches his mouth away from mine long enough to yell, "Fuck off, losers," before reclaiming it. There's more laughing outside and a voice that is definitely Linus's calls, "I hope you're properly servicing our champion!" but it's a little more distant than the voices had been before and there's a clear shuffling on the stairs and the sound of someone else—Keith or Lucas, maybe—saying, "Move it, pervs."

I slump against Chase. "Well, that's kind of a mood killer."

"Is it?" He kisses me, clearly not bothered in the slightest.

The truth is, I don't know. I hate that they make me sound like a groupie, but isn't that what I am? What I've always been? Didn't I sit in the bleachers for years just watching, cheering, being a fangirl of this guy who barely said hi in the halls until this year?

Didn't I have fantasies of "servicing the champion" late at night in my room, in the bathtub?

Isn't every bit of this exactly what I wanted?

"Maybe not," I say, hoping it sounds like a genuine concession. I don't *want* it to be a mood killer. I want us to be on the same page. I want this to feel real. I spent so much time fantasizing and I get to make it come true if I want to.

It's so much power.

I just wish it felt like power I still wanted.

In a flash, I think of Gia, how she makes her dreams happen—whatever they are. How she does the thing and hopes emotions will follow, and they usually do. I can do that. I can do the thing. I can do the thing and feel what I want to feel, what I'm probably just too self-conscious to feel.

"I don't know if I'm properly 'servicing the champion,'" I say, tapping his lower lip.

"Again, not something I was counting on happening tonight."

"I know." And I do. "But say I wanted to."

His eyebrows rise a fraction. "Do you?"

I've always wanted to, I think, but it's a weird answer and a weird non-answer all at the same time, so I kiss down his chest instead, figuring that'll say everything I need.

His breath hitches as I get to the top of his jeans and slowly undo the button, and it's quiet enough for me to hear that there's still hollering coming in our direction, but it must be from downstairs. I wish we'd put on music or something, but it'd seemed so loud earlier that it wasn't necessary.

Now all I hear is my own heartbeat pulsing in my ears and Chase's shallow, rapidly increasing breaths as we take the "high scorer" title to a whole new level. For as much as he doesn't care what other people hear or don't, he bites into a pillow rather than screaming out, and it takes away any doubt I might've had about whether he's worth taking this leap.

"Holy shit," he breathes when we're done.

So, not bad for my first time on a guy, then. Apparently

the reading up on it I used to do in preparation of this moment paid off. Good to know.

"Do I get your MVP trophy now?" I ask.

He laughs, still weak as he relaxes against the pillows. "For now. But you have to give me the chance to earn it back."

His gaze flickers over my short skirt and it takes me a minute to realize what he's saying.

One of Shannon's rules was never to go down on a guy because it gives them all the power and they never reciprocate, which Gia reluctantly confirmed was true, though she definitely did it all the time anyway. Kiki had just snorted, and I'd pretended I was taking notes, as usual, though I'd been thinking, *Good—I wouldn't want him to. Way too many guys talk about how gross it is and I don't ever want Chase to look at me that way.*

Shannon's proving to be wrong; reciprocating clearly isn't an issue for Chase, not with the way he's eyeing me. And it's also clear he isn't gonna find it—or me—gross. But . . . I still don't want him to do it. It's never been part of my Chase fantasy.

And, okay, maybe I'm not ready to have my memory of the one time someone *did* go down on me replaced, especially since it's clear that's never happening with Jasmine again.

Maybe.

"We've got plenty of time for that in the future," I say, giving him a quick kiss. "How about we go downstairs before those guys come back and harass us again? Besides, you should spend some time at your own party."

He looks disappointed for a moment, but only that.

"True—we've always got Homecoming. I can get a room, if you want."

From zero expectations to a room at Homecoming in the space of one blow job. Noted.

My thoughts must show on my face because he quickly adds, "No pressure."

"I'll think about it," I promise as he retrieves our clothes from the floor and tosses me my shirt. And I'm sure that I will, nonstop.

"Cool."

We get dressed and cleaned up, and he makes a little teasing "aw" of disappointment as I scrub off the last of the paint in the Ferrises' enormous en suite bathroom. "You ready?" I ask as soon as I've reapplied lip gloss, a futile attempt to make myself look put together despite my clothes having the permanently rumpled look of someone who's just rolled around with her new boyfriend.

"Ready." He holds out a hand and I take it, amazed at how quickly and comfortably we've slipped into these roles, and then he opens the door.

The picture of the crown with a big number 14 on it is still there, but no one else is; they're all crowded in the living room, being serenaded by what I immediately recognize as Gia on karaoke. Taylor Swift is her go-to. In addition to being a huge fangirl, she has no problem hitting the notes, but her performance always falls a little flat because she doesn't have the romantic angst; very few of those lyrics work when you're smiling happily at your boyfriend through them. Currently, she's warbling her way through "Blank Space," singing it at a starry-eyed Tommy as if it's a wedding-worthy romance rather than an epic burn of a song.

Chase's teammates spot us immediately and come over to give him shit, but he tells them to mind their business and find their own girls so they can stop worrying what he's up to with his. Then he raises a fist and cheers loudly for Gia, and I squeeze him around the waist as I watch her cheeks light up with pleasure.

He really is a good guy. Hot as hell, and I feel safe with him. I genuinely like him, a lot.

That's what matters, right? Not that I didn't want to go further tonight?

God, I wish I could talk to Shannon. I know she's here, but I doubt her brain's been *here* here since five minutes after she walked through the door. She's just so good at being blunt with her advice, and that's exactly what I need—not Gia's effusive and all-consuming belief that love is always the answer, or Kiki's comfort in the form of dismissing all high school romance as temporary bullshit. I need some real talk, Shannon Salter style, even if it means sitting through a lecture on breaking one of her rules, complete with an *I told you so*, even though this isn't what she told me at all.

And suddenly, there she is, on the "stage," taking the mic from Gia as "Blank Space" fades out and everyone applauds. I'm stunned to see Shannon standing next to the machine. She *never* participates in karaoke, or anything else that might make her look silly. Even Kiki participates in karaoke more than Shannon, as long as you let her sing angry 90s girl rock. But maybe Shannon's been practicing or something. I know better than anyone how much time she puts into making everything she does look effortless. And she certainly looks the part of a pop star in her sequined miniskirt, a purchase I don't recognize.

A purchase that means she's been shopping without me.

I don't have any time to dwell on how her friendship is slipping away from me before Shannon hits me with the next blow. "And now," she says in her most tantalizing I-am-the-first-to-everything voice, "for the first time in Stratford history, please welcome the vocal stylings of . . . Jasmine Killary!"

She's joking. She has to be. When did Jasmine even get here? But sure enough, there she is, stepping up to the mic and laughing with Shannon as everyone cheers. Her hair is in a glossy high ponytail that swirls around her shoulders—shoulders bared by cutouts in her skin-colored dress and glittering with a dusting of gold. I'm too short to see anything else, but she's head-to-head with Shannon so she must be wearing at least three-inch heels.

She's dressed to get every single eye in the room on her, and it's working.

I couldn't take mine off her if I tried.

The music starts—Shannon must've flipped it on—and my brain is such a blur it takes me a few seconds to figure out what song she chose. But there's a *lot* of whistling from the hornier members of the football team who do know.

And, with the first word, it clicks.

Demi Lovato's "Cool for the Summer," a fucking *anthem* for girls exploring each other's bodies.

Jasmine's low, sexy voice can't hit Demi's higher notes, but she's singing about fooling around with a girl and absolutely nobody gives a shit about her vocal skills. Behind me, even Chase is whistling, his hands on my shoulders, ironically the only thing to keep me steady when my body wants to shake uncontrollably. Every lyric cuts me like a knife, and I wait for her to make eye contact, to tell me to my face that she's reducing our summer to a little curiosity, but she never does.

Instead, she goes all in, flirting with what feels like literally everyone else in the audience. Thanks to Shannon's proximity, people are whispering, coming up with their own interpretations, even as Jasmine practically sits in Paulie Wolman's lap. Everything about this is awful, except that it isn't. Watching her perform is incredible, and when I close my eyes, her voice strokes me the way her fingers used to. I'm a horrible person, standing with my boyfriend and completely melting at a girl's voice, at the memory of her touch. To make it worse, I suspect—though you can never know with Jasmine—this song was chosen to tell me to fuck all the way off and give up trying to have any semblance of a connection with her, that any deeper meaning to this summer was entirely in my head.

"She's good, huh?" Chase murmurs in my ear, dropping his elbows onto my shoulders, lightly brushing a hand against my boob as if he knows watching Jasmine is turning me inside out, making me want to be touched.

That it's making me want what being alone with him upstairs didn't.

That I'm more attracted to Jasmine, to this girl who seems to hate me, than I am to my incredible boyfriend.

All at once, way too much crashes into place.

Chapter Fifteen

THEN

It was Declan's idea to host a low country boil, to persuade my mom to finally eat some local cuisine. My mom grew up on Russian fare—pelmeni, pirozhki, borscht, and all manner of things made with potatoes, cabbage, and/or sour cream. She'll eat fish eggs before she'll eat a prawn that's still got its head on. So, it's been kind of a struggle for her spending the summer in an area dominated by seafood and barbecue. (Though she loves that the Outer Banks has somehow become a hot spot for Eastern European students to work for the summer. Getting to speak Russian to people who aren't me or her parents has been the highlight of her summer, I think.) Naturally, Declan sees that as a challenge.

My mother is not amused.

And because he can't ask my mother to plan a social

event she'd rather die than attend, it's up to me and Jasmine (and okay, hired staff) to get everything going.

"I wish you could see your hair right now!" Jasmine laughs as we struggle to weigh down the gingham-printed tablecloths against the breeze rolling off the Atlantic.

"You encouraged this hair!" I lift my hand self-consciously to my new blond curls. I'm still getting used to the way they dance in the breeze, so much lighter than the inches of mousy gold I left on the cutting room floor of the Seaside Salon. But between the way my new hair frames my face and the deep tan I'm getting out in the Carolina sun, my eyes pop blue-green more than ever, and I look healthy and happy and *different*.

Jasmine did a photo shoot of me immediately afterward, but I keep stopping short of posting any of the pictures. I don't want anyone's opinions yet. I like that it's something that's strictly Larissa of the Outer Banks— Tinkerbell, if you will. Something separate from Stratford. Shannon would completely kill me if she knew, but Shannon's in Paris, posting selfies from beneath the Arc de Triomphe and at little cafés dotting the city. She's having her version of a fabulous summer, and somewhere along the way, I realized that I am too. I may not be scarfing pain au chocolate on the Champs-Elysées or whatever, but I don't envy it. I'm about to eat my weight in shrimp, crab, clams, lobster, and corn, and I feel great about that.

"I'm not making fun of the hair under *normal* circumstances," Jasmine clarifies, smoothing one of her perfect pigtail braids. "It's just kind of . . . everywhere right now. I'm sure it'll look lovely for the party."

"I'm sure your *face* will look lovely for the party," I shoot back, feeling childish as I kick sand in front of me, being careful not to land any of it on the white plastic folding chairs.

"Was that supposed to be a burn?" Jasmine finishes placing shells on her corners of the table, then does a cartwheel in the sand, her mint-green-polished toes pointing elegantly at the sun. "Pathetic, Tinkerbell."

"*You're* pathetic." I drop the rest of my shells in a messy cluster and start my own run—roundoff, back handspring, back tuck. Being a former cheerleader has its merits.

"Holy shit." Jasmine's jaw drops. "What did you just do?"

"Oh, did I not mention that I used to be on the cheer-leading squad?" I blow on my nails.

"You're *joking*. Show me again."

I do, even though it makes me dizzy. It's worth it for the way she wolf whistles when I'm done and yells, "That's so hot!" In truth, my form is completely off, and Gia would have so many words for how out of practice I am, but I love that Jasmine thinks I'm amazing exactly as I am.

"I can't believe I didn't know you could do that," she says, wiping away the sweat that lightly beads her forehead.

I shrug like it's no big deal. "There's a lot you don't know about me."

"Oh, I don't know if that's true." A little smile plays

on her lips as she bends to draw her name in the sand. "Let's see . . . I know your favorite color is turquoise. I know your favorite author is Clementine Walker. And I know you take your iced coffee with caramel syrup and way too much sugar."

"Anyone who follows me on Snapchat knows those things."

"Okay." She stands and dusts off her hands, crosses her arms over her chest. "I know you used to spend summers at your mom's friend's house in the Finger Lakes, and that's where you had your first kiss. I know the only two things guaranteed to make you cry are dogs dying in movies and the smell of salami and eggs, the second because it's the only thing your shitty father ever made right. And I know you're writing a romance novel in that notebook you keep under your pillow, even though you won't let anyone read it. How am I doing?"

"Not bad," I concede, giving my sternum a quick press with my palm to try and break up the weirdness building beneath it. "But I know you too. I know you've tried exactly six times to replicate your steta's kibbeh recipe, and that it's what you'd choose as your last meal on death row. I know your name was one of your parents' biggest fights, because your mom wanted to name you after said grandmother and your father straight-up refused. I know you still sleep with a stuffed panda oh-so-cleverly named Panda. And I know you're scared of waterskiing but don't want anyone to know, because you don't like people knowing you have any fears at all."

Her eyes widen. "I am *not*—"

"Yeah, you are."

She exhales. "Yeah, I am. How the hell did you know that?"

I watch you. I can't freaking stop watching you. Wanna know some more things I know? That you have a lightning bolt of beauty marks on the back of your left thigh. That nothing tastes better than sparkling apple cider on your tongue in the hot tub. That every time I hear you reading French aloud to practice for the AP exam, I have to take a cold shower.

"Just very brilliant," I say with a shrug.

She snorts. "Apparently. Come on, let's go husk the corn."

I jump at the chance to clear my head of the thoughts I definitely shouldn't be having and follow her into the kitchen, where green piles await us on the center island's concrete countertop. We immediately get to attacking it, yanking down the leaves and stringy silks and snapping them off at the base. Before long there's a huge pile of garbage heaped in front of us on the counter, but it smells so sweet and delicious, I want to dive right in.

"You look like you wanna go to town on that," Jasmine says dryly as we scoop up the mess. "Just remember, it's still raw."

"Okay, but I'm starving," I grumble.

"We're doing guacamole next." She opens the fridge and pulls out a bunch of herbs while I grab the avocados. "I promise not to tell if you sneak an avocado or twelve."

"That's the kindest offer you've ever made me."

"Probably."

Together we peel and pit until our fingers are stained

green. I'm about to suggest a break when something cool and slimy smushes against my face.

"Did you *just*." I whirl around to see a smirk on Jasmine's face and a mashed avocado slice in her hand. "Oh, no you did not." I grab an avocado half and leap in her direction, but she's half a step too fast and we end up in a running battle.

"Gotta be way faster than that, Tinkerbell!" she crows, and in the second she stops to gloat, I wrap an arm around her waist and mash the avocado into her head.

"My hair!" she shrieks, even though we both need to shower before the party.

She rolls out of my grasp as I gleefully hold up my green hands and say, "Avocado oil is healthy for it! You're welcome, Princess!"

"I'll show you a princess." She comes charging toward me and tackles me to the floor, each of us trying to smear the other's face with goop.

"This is *not* what I thought you meant when you told me I could sneak an avocado," I growl.

"Oh, I'm sorry." She sits up and holds her hands in the air, but she's still pinning me down, her knees holding tight to my waist. Even covered in green gunk, her cutoff tee a stained and sweaty mess, she manages to look sexy as hell. "Go ahead."

"Don't mind if I do." I take one of those hands and bring it to my lips, licking the traces of avocado from her palm. She laughs, but her giggles taper off as I suck one finger at a time into my mouth.

By the time I'm done tasting each one, the look in Jasmine's golden eyes could melt the corn off its cobs. I'm about to make a move when Declan's voice rings through the kitchen. "Girls? Did you do the guacamole?"

Jasmine rolls off me quick as lightning and I jump up, just as Declan walks into the kitchen. Even though we haven't been caught flirting, we've sure as hell been caught making a mess of his pristine kitchen. I watch as he takes in the sight, both of us covered in avocado that should be mashed into his carefully chosen stone bowls, and his mouth quirks into a grin.

"So, not done yet, I see."

"Uh, no, sir."

Jasmine snorts. I have not called Declan "sir" once the entire summer. In fact, I have carefully avoided referring to him as anything at all, except to thank him for having me. And when I did call him Mr. Killary, he immediately told me to call him Declan.

I did not.

"There's still time," he says with a wink, and he walks out.

"Uh, no, sir," Jasmine mocks me, and I elbow her in the side. She bursts out laughing, and so do I, and we get to work.

It takes us twenty minutes of working side by side, with zero fooling around, to finish and clean up enough not to leave a gross mess for the crew that'll be taking care of it at the end of the night. By the time we head to our respective showers, I positively reek.

As I scrub the smells of onion, garlic, and bell pepper from my skin, I can't help thinking how funny it is that Jasmine comes off as the most dauntingly sophisticated seventeen-year-old girl on the planet, but when it's only us, she's somebody else entirely. She's playful and warm and has the patience of a saint when she's teaching me about exposures and light meters and how to get the best angles in selfies. She's like her dad in her excitement to get me to try new things, and like her mom in how much joy she gets from fashion, makeup, and styling. Yesterday, she finally pulled me into her closet and demanded I let her give me some things she never wears, things she swears are too small, and before I know it, I'm wearing an entirely new outfit from earrings to anklet. (Her having dinky-size feet like mine was too much to hope for, unfortunately.)

And later at night, especially nights when Mom and Declan are at events, or traveling to meetings, or even nights where Mom passes out early and Declan locks himself in his suite, far away from the rest of us . . . those nights show me something else entirely.

We inevitably end up in her bed, curled around one another and playing with each other's fingers or giving each other chills until one of us finds an excuse to place a kiss on the other. It's agony, waiting until I can figure out how to get away with it, or waiting for her to, waiting, waiting, waiting until we can explain it away with sleepiness or drunkenness or just wanting the other one to feel and taste how amazing this new lip gloss is.

I've started to think about them in advance, how I might excuse dropping a kiss on this one spot on her neck that always elicits this tiny noise that makes my toes curl. It isn't quite a moan and it isn't quite a growl and as soon as I hear it, I'm out of my mind for the rest of the night.

Maybe tonight we can pick up where we left off. If I can get a dab of guac on her throat, I can watch her close her eyes as I lick it off. Hear that sound she makes as I lick again for good measure. And again. Maybe I gently suck at her throat, the way I did the other night. Judging by the way she pressed against me, by the way I can still feel the pressure of her fingertips below my waist, the way I could just barely hear her begging me to do it again . . .

Images come to mind of sliding off her shirt—for easier access to that spot, of course. Of taking mine off, which only makes sense. Who wants a rough cotton shirt against your skin when someone else's skin feels so much better? And her skin is *so* soft, scented with that peach lotion, and—

I don't even realize what I've been doing until my nails scrape the tile of the shower, trying to find something to hold onto while my body shudders around my fingers. I grasp the indentation in the wall meant to hold soap and promise myself that I'll think about how messed-up this is later, after I'm done feeling so, so good.

True to my word, I feel like a mess when I dry myself off after the shower. I don't know how else to describe it because I don't feel *gross*, exactly—it's not like I think there's anything wrong with masturbating (or, let's be real, like it's my first time), or with finding a girl attractive. I just feel confused. And guilty. This is how I think about Chase; it isn't how I'm supposed to be thinking about Jasmine. It isn't how she'd *want* me to think about her. God, if she knew what'd happened, she'd probably never touch me again.

I wish I was okay with that.

I'm supposed to be okay with that.

It's something we do for fun, not something I think about in the shower or feel down to my bones. It's not something we do with *intention*.

But isn't that what you were just doing, by thinking about how to make it happen? my brain nags. *You were trying to plan it, and the whole point is that this is a thing that only occasionally happens between you two.*

Except it's not occasional.

When did it stop being occasional?

It's too much. It's messing with my brain. I already have my shower rotation all worked out, and it fully involves a certain number fourteen football player. There isn't any more space for those kinds of thoughts. Chase has been serving me just fine for years now.

Anyway, nothing's going to happen tonight. All our friends are coming to the boil, as are Declan's, and knowing my mom, she invited some of her new Russian friends. The house and beach will be packed, and maybe somewhere in there will be a new guy to entertain myself with—someone who makes sense, who'll be a perfect placeholder until I'm back in Chase's orbit.

I feel firm in this plan as I go full country girl, tying

a sleeveless gingham shirt (thanks, Jasmine) under my boobs and pairing it with cutoff shorts. I'll have to cover up once the evening hits, but for now, I look cute and summery and up for a good time. I style my curls exactly how they taught me to at Seaside and add only the tiniest touch of makeup since I've yet to find an affordable mascara that stays true to the word "waterproof" when faced with parties on the beach.

I'm putting in the gold hoops my mom bought me for my sweet sixteen when my mom walks in. "Oh, Larotchka. You look so cute. Someone you're trying to impress coming tonight?"

"I hope so," I say with a smile. "But you're still in your work clothes! People are gonna start showing up soon."

"I know, I know." She drops her bag on the bed and fans herself. "I can't even think about what I'm wearing until I take a shower. They say New York summers are bad, but this heat is unbearable."

"Missing your dreamy winters of twenty below zero?" I tease her.

"Ha ha," she says, pronouncing the h's with the hard Russian *kh*. "Clearly you have your father's sense of humor."

She always does that, brings him up strictly for the sake of crafting insults. I've gotten so used to it that I barely notice. But tonight, my head swimming with confusion about romance and relationships, I have a thousand questions about him and them that I know she'll never answer.

Then again, he was a he, so how much would it really help?

Before I can ask something coherent, she slips into the bathroom for her much-needed shower, leaving me to collapse on the bed with a self-pitying groan.

We're only messing around. I know that. I'm eternally obsessed with Chase Harding, and I assume Jasmine is still hooking up with Carter, in those rare instances where I lose her at parties or on the beach. It's not that I think there's more happening, it's just . . .

Just what?

That's your problem, Shannon would say. *You can't accept a "just." You think you can, but you always need to know what's past that, and sometimes, there's nothing.*

Maybe talking to Shannon is exactly what I need. She may give way too much advice, and sometimes it's downright bad, but not always. Sometimes it's exactly what I need to hear, enough that I hear it even when she's thousands of miles away. I light up my phone to check the time and do a quick calculation to see if it's too late to call.

It's about one in the morning in Paris, which is sort of on the border of acceptable, but what would I say? *Hey, Shan—I've been hooking up with this girl and I'm confused about what it means?* How would she know, without knowing Jasmine?

Maybe imaginary Shannon's advice is right, though. Sometimes "just" is exactly that. Jasmine and I are just having fun. It's not even like things are happening intentionally; they just *happen* when we're doing other things. What could be more "just" than that?

Satisfied, I do one last touch-up of my makeup, take a selfie, and pick up the newest Clementine Walker book.

Who needs tough love when you can escape into pure fluff?

Half an hour later, the boil is in full swing, and guests are swarming the gingham-covered tables piled high with jumbo shrimp, crawfish, sausage, crab, and corn. The air smells salty and briny and spicy and sweet, and my mouth is watering, even though I'm secretly scared of the crawfish and their freaky heads.

"Are you coming or what?" Jasmine calls from the table where she's sitting with Keisha, Brea, Derek, and Owen, glass bottles of colorful wine coolers dotting the cloth in front of them. "Where have you been?"

I'd gotten too wrapped up in my book, which is embarrassing since I'd already read it once this summer. I only looked up from it because Gia FaceTimed me from cheer camp, which she does every week to show me what I'm missing by dropping off the squad, and by the time we hung up, everyone was here and the food was out of the pots and on the table.

"Friend called" is all I offer as I grab a plate and sit my butt in one of the white plastic chairs, my eyes roving hungrily over the selection. Sausage is an easy choice—you don't grow up the granddaughter of Tolya Bogdan without kolbasa being one of your major food groups. I glance at my mom and see she had the same idea. Declan is sitting next to her and laughing as he gestures to the other food.

"You're missing some damn good crawfish," says Keisha, plucking one from the pile and cracking it open so quickly I can't even see how she's doing it. "They don't make 'em like this in DC. Best part of coming here for the summers."

"And that's from someone who doesn't even eat it right," says Derek, picking up one of the bright red creepers, twisting it, and—oh God, is he sucking something right out of the shell?

"Drinking the juice is so gross." Brea wrinkles her nose. "Keisha eats it the normal way."

"The juice is the best part!" Jasmine protests, and it's dizzying watching them all attack the pile with different methods. There's twisting and pulling and cracking and drinking and biting and loud savoring, but I can't follow any of it; I help myself to the clams instead.

Clearly, I'm not very subtle. "Are you not even gonna try them?" Jasmine asks, eyeing my plate as if it's got nothing but plain white rice on it.

"I'm good," I say. I'm not about to admit that I don't know how to eat them.

"Don't tell me you're scared of them like your mom."

"Hey, leave my mom out of this." I wave a hand dismissively. "The clams and sausage are delicious."

Brea sighs. "Sugar, you're from New York. There's no crime in being a Yankee who doesn't know how to eat crawfish. Just admit it."

My face flames, but the others smirk and eat another one each, building the pile of shells in the bowl in front of us.

Jasmine laughs. "Come on, I'll show you. Pick one up."

I watch her fingers as she carefully pries the shell from the fish, mint polish catching the sunlight. I grab one and try to replicate her movements, but I end up squishing it in my hands and shrieking in surprise.

Everyone else cracks up, but Jasmine grins and says, "Okay, let's at least make sure you get to taste it." She tips the shell holding the juice into my mouth, and I'm determined not to be grossed out. It actually *is* good, in fact, especially followed by the fish itself, which she frees and holds for me to eat from her fingertips.

"*Fine*, that's good," I concede, "but I'm clearly not up to cracking them open myself."

"I've got you covered." Jasmine opens another and feeds it to me the same way, and we laugh as I manage to spill on myself. After a while, we get into a messy rhythm, and I can't even count how many the five of us eat as the sun sinks below the horizon.

By the time the party dies down and cleanup begins, I feel like a beached whale, but it's worth it. This might be the most fun I've had the entire summer. I miss my friends, but the ones I've made here are so awesome, it's impossible to wish I'd chosen cheer camp with Gia, or be jealous of Shannon's trip to Paris or Kiki's to Japan, and I'm certainly no longer wishing I were dusting off shelves at the Book and Bean.

Keisha and Owen even stay to help clean up. Keisha and I are clearing glasses and cans from the table when she says, "You two are cute."

I cock my head. "Who two?"

Her eyebrow rises all the way up. "Seriously?"

A billion crawfish slosh in my stomach, swimming in apple-flavored wine cooler. I don't know why, but I want to hear her say it out loud, maybe so I can stop feeling

delusional. But I already played clueless, and to acknowledge that I know who she's referring to is to acknowledge
that I see something too. Which is not an option. I shrug
instead.

She rolls her eyes, but lets it go. She's certainly had
enough annoying experience with people trying to pair
her up. "Do you think you'll come back next summer?
Or is this a one-time thing for you and your mom?"

It hadn't occurred to me that we might never do this
again. But then, I haven't really given much thought to
this ending, life going back to the status quo. It's too hard
to imagine waking up in a home that isn't filled with the
sound of Jasmine tunelessly humming her favorite indie rock songs, or going to parties where no one's taking
bets on how many drinks it'll take Owen to challenge
someone to a dance-off. (He always loses. He's a horrible dancer, whereas Jack's classically trained in ballet,
Brea's so flexible her body moves like liquid, and Keisha's number one goal after declaring a computer science
major her sophomore year is to join the Georgetown
step team.)

Could I be part of this group for real? I think I'd like
to be. I love my friends at home—how much fun we
have and how much we push each other and are there
for each other—but here I feel like . . . I get to be and do
other things. I don't have to know exactly who I am and
what I want. I'm a summer girl, living my highlight reel.
Maybe I don't want anything realer than that.

But, much like I didn't have a choice this summer, I
won't next time either.

"Depends on my mom's job," I say, already afraid to

get too attached to the idea. "But I'd like to. I like hanging out with you guys."

A small, knowing smile tugs at her lips that says, "Yeah, I know who you like hanging out with." And even though it's absurd and terrible, I want her to press the issue one more time, out loud, to tell me we look like something even though I don't know if I want us to look like something. But Keisha's not that person, and we finish cleaning the table in silence.

NOW

I make an excuse to leave the party and pull out my phone as I steal into the backyard. I've only spoken to Keisha a few times since the summer—commenting on each other's selfies, a group chat to tell us she made the step team so we could send every celebratory emoji in existence—but I call her without hesitation. I don't want to have this conversation without hearing her tone of voice.

"Hey, girl," she greets me, instantly transporting me back to the deck of her parents' house, to afternoons spent playing spades and hearts over sweet tea and messing around in her closet with Brea and Jasmine while she played Fortnite with some friend from school. "What's up?"

The question that'd been dancing on the tip of my tongue dies. "Long time, no speak," I say, despite it being one of my most hated phrases. "I'm at a party and I was thinking of you. Thought I'd say hi."

It's not a *total* lie, anyway.

"Ooh, is that the same party Jasmine's at? It looks like fun!"

I blink slowly. "How did you know Jasmine's here?"

"I helped her pick an outfit over FaceTime, and I just saw her karaoke performance on IG Live. That was hot."

You have no idea. Just like *I* had no idea they spoke so often in the off season. So much for baring my soul to Keisha. "Did you know she was transferring here?"

"I mean, it was a pretty last-minute decision, so I didn't know until the night before. All she told me was that her mom was selling their house and moving up near family, so they figured it'd make more sense for her to be at the same school all year. It was a little weird that her mom wouldn't just wait until after graduation, but Jas seemed cool about it. Anyway, you'd know better than I would."

You'd think. So many secrets. So many questions.

I sidestep that. I don't want her to know that I don't know, that my closeness with Jasmine this past summer was some sort of temporary thing, tied to the tide or whatever. "Well, I assume that since we're both up here, that means we can get you up for a visit."

Keisha laughs. "You know I had this conversation with Jasmine like two hours ago, right? Y'all coordinate this coercion or what?"

"You know we did," I lie, because I don't know how to explain why we wouldn't have. "Does that mean you're thinking about it?"

"I am. Trying to work a few things out, but I'll let y'all know."

I'm surprised to find that the idea of Keisha coming to visit dislodges something in my chest and makes it a little easier to breathe. Seeing Keisha again would be like getting a piece of my summer back, connecting that part of me to current me in a way that seeing Jasmine only tears apart.

It's been a long time since I've felt like myself, I realize. Maybe seeing Keisha will bring that back.

Maybe it'll bring me and Jasmine back to normal too.

Whatever that is.

Chapter Sixteen

It's an unusually slow morning at the Book and Bean, and I can't drink any more failed latte art, so I do something I've been both itching to do and dreading.

I pick up the book I started writing this summer.

I'd tried to sit at my laptop in the beach house but typing on a computer made the attempt too real, so I'd bought a flamingo-patterned spiral notebook at some cheesy tourist shop, planted myself in a chaise by the pool, and wrote. But I didn't get far. It was a silly, rambling story about a guy named Oliver and a girl named Jillian who meet on the beach in—where else—the Outer Banks and hit it off, only to learn they're living in the same house for the summer. Unfortunately, after that initial "Oh no!" moment, I completely ran out of plot, so I put the notebook away and forgot about it.

But after talking to Keisha last night, it hits me— Oliver and Jillian aren't alone in the house. They have roommates. At least two of them. As soon as that comes to me, those characters start to draw themselves in my brain, and I introduce Andrew, a lifeguard who has his pick of the ladies, and Nadia, because of course I had to write a Russian girl. Nadia's working as a waitress and perpetually smells like fried shrimp, so much so that Jillian has to look twice to realize that with her impossibly long legs and white-blond hair, Nadia's stunning.

My pen pauses on the page. Why would it matter that Nadia's stunning when Oliver's the love interest? Hmm, maybe Jillian's jealous, nervous that Oliver will gravitate toward her instead? No, I don't see Jillian as insecure, and I definitely don't want some girl-hate scenario . . . I make sure they have a friendly encounter, and grin as I write Nadia breaking out into some Russian swears as she drops her coffee mug.

"You might want to work on those skills before you start your job," Jillian warns her, voice filled with teasing warmth. "I don't think that's how customers generally prefer to get free refills."

My phone beeps, and I tear myself from my notebook to look at the screen.

Spoke to Keisha last night. Says she spoke to you about coming to visit.

It's the first text I've received from Jasmine since she replied with a heart emoji to the goodbye text I sent her from the airport in Norfolk. It's still visible in the chain. I could scroll up and see pages and pages of proof that we were more than we feel like now.

But I don't.

My entire body goes cold at the sight of her name, at the taunting red heart. What the fuck *was* that song last night? *I'm* the one with a boyfriend. I've *clearly* moved on. Why the hell does she need to sing to me in front of an entire room of *my* friends—*my friends*, no matter what sort of bond is happening between her and Shannon—that it was only a stupid summer game? *I know. I have a boyfriend.*

And neither she nor my boyfriend ever needs to know how I felt hearing that song, or how I felt watching her onstage, or how I ran out to call Keisha because I wanted to hear from someone who once upon a time thought we looked like two people who liked each other. I fucking went *down* on Chase last night. I'm doing everything right. I'm doing all the things I'm supposed to be doing.

So why do I want to stand here and cry into glass bottles of flavored syrup?

Yep, I reply, blinking back the tears pinpricking my eyelids. *She said you mentioned it too. Great minds, I guess.*

Not a minute later, the reply comes. *Yeah, well, we'll let you know when we figure out a date.*

That's what Jasmine just had to text me about the day after that performance? She wanted to let me know I wouldn't be part of this planning conversation? God, I don't even know why I'm surprised by her bullshit anymore. If she wanted to talk, she could've come down here; she knows exactly where I am at 10:00 a.m. on a Saturday morning. Everyone does. And if she didn't wanna talk, well, I guess this is how she lets me know it.

Thanks, I guess, I think.

Thx is what I actually type.

I put my phone away and turn back to my notebook, happy to spend time with people who can't send me shitty text messages. It's easier than I expect to pick up where I left off. Nadia giving a teasing response to Jillian. Jillian playfully replying in Nadia's Russian accent, then asking her to teach her those swear words. At some point as I write, I realize I've left Oliver out of the story, and I messily add that Jillian is talking to Nadia while waiting for The Guy to show his face again.

I'm on a serious roll when I'm suddenly interrupted by fingers waving over my page. I look up, blinking into the light as I remember I'm at work, and am startled to see Chase standing there, hazel eyes twinkling as he laughs. "What's got you so busy? I called your name like three times. Are you late on an assignment?"

Well, I guess The Guy has arrived. "Just something for fun." I close the notebook reluctantly and tuck it under the counter. "What brings you to the Book and Bean? Have you heard about our stunning latte art?"

"Hmm, I do recall a beautiful girl I was at a party with last night mentioning something about that. Thought I should see for myself, and maybe see if the barista was up for throwing in a kiss."

A kiss sounds like the perfect way to forget all this stupid drama, and I stand on my toes and pull Chase down by his collar, closing the height gap between us as I press my lips to his. I kiss him with all the force of my anger and confusion at Jasmine and the want for him I had for so damn long.

When we break apart, he looks a little bit like a

cartoon character who's just been hit with a mallet, stars and birdies flying around his head.

He looks like I wish I felt. But all I really feel is that I can't wait to finish the scene between Jillian and Nadia.

By Monday morning, I feel like I'm gonna explode if I don't talk to someone about what's going on in my head. I go through the pros and cons of talking to my mom, to Shannon, to Kiki, to Gia, but I can't imagine having this conversation with any of them. I don't really know where my mom stands on same-sex relationship stuff, but it isn't exactly smiled upon in the motherland. I tell her just about everything, but considering it involves her boss's daughter, I need a little more certainty before I drop this particular bomb.

As for the others . . . even if they were chill about that—and I feel pretty confident at least Shannon and Kiki would be, if not Gia, who comes from a super traditional family—none of them would take being lied to all semester very well. And maybe Kiki already knows something and maybe she doesn't, but her podcast is more popular than ever, and I don't know that I can trust her to keep quiet.

When I walk into AP Enviro, I'm hit by the most obvious answer in the world.

"Hey, partner," I say as I take my seat next to Jamie. "How was your weekend?"

"Good!" Her face brightens. "I took Taylor into the city on Friday night to see their favorite band—I got tickets for their birthday. Had a great time. You? I assume you went to Ferris's party."

"I did. It was fun," I say automatically, knowing that there's no way the expression on my face matches the glow on hers when she talks about her date with Taylor. But she's given me an opening, and I need to take it before the bell rings. "Typical. Not quite the same as a world-class date." I wiggle my eyebrows and she laughs.

"Yeah, well, dates are more our thing than parties, anyway. The fewer people we know, the better."

"I hear that," I say, even though it's generally the opposite of my philosophy. "Did you know that about each other when you started dating? And how did you two start dating, anyway?"

It's not the smoothest transition, but it's not hard to get Jamie to talk about Taylor. I've asked her about her weekend most Monday mornings, and for most of the last six months, Taylor's factored somewhere into her answer. "They took someone's spot in our weekly DnD game, and after a couple of weeks of crushing on them, I just . . . gave them a set of nonbinary dice I saw online and that was it. Probably the gutsiest dating move I've ever made, honestly."

It is, but that's not the part I'm focused on. "But there was no, like . . . question of whether . . ." I trail off, unsure how to phrase the rest.

"I was already out as bi, and they were out as pan and nonbinary, if that's what you mean. Not that it has to mean they were attracted to *me*, but I knew I wasn't ruled out or anything."

"Yeah, that," I say, grateful she knew what I was

going for, even as her answer makes my cheeks feel hot. "So, you've been out for a long time?" She's been out the whole time I've known her, but she only moved to Stratford from Connecticut two years ago.

"Oh, yeah. Since, like, fifth grade. And even then, it's not like I really needed to come out. My room was a shrine to Wonder Woman and I don't even read comics." She grins. "Wasn't tough for my mom and stepdad to read between the lines."

"And Taylor?"

"Pretty much the same. They introduced themselves with their pronouns the instant we met, so I've never known them to ID as anything else."

Well, that was lovely for the two of them, but not particularly helpful for me.

Or maybe it is. Maybe this is making clear that I'm blowing things way out of proportion. If being bi means always knowing, well, that isn't me. The only girls on my bedroom walls are my friends, and I'm certainly not into any of them that way.

That settles it. I'm straight. Just like I always thought.

I wait for the feeling of a weight lifting from my shoulders, but it never comes.

Chapter Seventeen

NOW

"Who has the highlighter?"

I pass the compact to Gia and get back to focusing on my eyebrows, which, despite having been waxed the day before, look like they could use another pluck or twelve. Or maybe they're overplucked. I can't keep up with eyebrow fashion.

"The liquid, not the powder," Gia says impatiently, and I shrug. Homecoming has arrived way too fast, and despite having a great dress with an awesomely poufy tulle skirt and enough sequins in the bodice to put the night sky to shame, I'm having an impossible time getting excited for the primping portion of the evening.

"Here, here." Kiki hands her the bottle and shoves me gently out of the way so she can examine her earring options in the mirror. "Which ones do you guys like better?"

I scrutinize her lobes. Kiki almost never swaps out the pearl studs her parents gave her for her seventeenth birthday, so it takes a second to adjust to anything sparkly in them. "The dangly ones are definitely more interesting, but the diamond studs are classy."

"Okay, so do I wanna be interesting or classy?" she asks, turning her head from side to side.

"You're always interesting," Shannon says sweetly. "Maybe try classy for once."

The rest of us crack up at her burn, including Kiki. "Better not mess with what's already working for me," she says, taking out the diamond and handing it to Shannon. "Classy is boring."

Shannon puts the studs back in her jewelry box, this massive antique thing her parents bought her for getting a five on the AP U.S. History exam. Half her room is filled with little trophies like that—a Kate Spade bag for her first all-A report card, a fancy ballerina painting for landing the principal role in her fifth-grade recital, a pair of Louboutins from when her team came in first in Model UN. To her credit, Shannon always shares— diamond studs, pricey makeup, and even the fancy barrette I'm wearing to hold my curls off my face.

"I bet your date will look classy," Shannon says, sweeping a minuscule clump of mascara from her otherwise perfect lashes.

I snort. "By date do you mean the podcast app on her phone?"

The other three girls exchange glances. "Pretty sure she means her actual date," says Gia, carefully rubbing the liquid highlighter onto her browbones.

"I'm sorry, what?" I cross my arms over my chest, the pink sequins that cover the strapless bodice digging into my skin. "Since when do *you*, Akiko Takayama, have a *date*? And how am I only hearing this five seconds before we get into the limo?"

"It's no big deal, drama queen," she says with a snort. "I'm going with Jasmine."

Hmm, I thought my hearing was OK, but it's clear something is malfunctioning, because there's no way that I was just informed on the night of the dance that Jasmine Killary is going to be in my limo as one of my best friends' dates. "I'm sorry, you're going with *who*?"

There's a collective whoosh of air intake as both Shannon and Gia suck in their breath. "Wow, Lar," says Gia, flicking an imaginary piece of dust from her silver cocktail dress, "it's the twenty-first century. This is really not a big deal."

It takes me a few seconds to realize that Gia fucking Peretti is giving *me* a lecture on homophobia, and this is all so twisted and ridiculous that I could die. Next to her, Shannon is shaking her head in similar disbelief and it takes everything in me not to scream.

How is this my life?

I exhale sharply and clap my hands together. "Okay, let's try this again. Kiki! I am very happy for you that you have a date! And it's cool that it's a girl! I just don't understand how the fact that you have a date—of any gender—somehow did not come up before now. With me, at least."

She shrugs. "It was kind of last minute, but she

wasn't going with anyone, and I was gonna be seventh-wheeling with you guys anyway, so."

"Great," I manage through gritted teeth.

Mercifully, the doorbell cuts through the tension filling the room and Gia squeals, effectively ending any conversation. We each take one last look at ourselves—and do one last lip gloss application—before heading out to the staircase to let our dates fully appreciate our glamorous descent.

"We're going as friends," Kiki murmurs just loud enough for me to hear, and I catch the flash of her smirk as she passes me so she can be the first to walk down.

Her words slash sharp and hot at my insides as the layers of her statement hit me.

Layer one: Kiki absolutely knows about my feelings for Jasmine, and maybe even knows about our history.

Layer two: Kiki put herself out there as queer to test the waters and wanted me to see that Shannon and Gia passed with flying colors.

But Kiki doesn't know about the party, the song, how Jasmine basically told me to fuck off in front of an entire room. She doesn't know how much deeper I got in with Chase. She's clearly more of a romantic than I thought, or at least a better friend, but even Stratford's greatest detective is missing some pretty important pieces to this case, and there's no filling them in now.

Especially when I reach the top of the stairs and see Jasmine standing at the bottom.

She looks . . . radiant. There's no other word for it. She's wearing a two-piece dress that's all glittering gold on top and matte on the bottom, short enough to show off long legs that glimmer with a little bit of that lotion I love. She's wearing a fancier set of gold bangles than usual and they match the earrings that march up her lobes. Even her eyes look like liquid gold, lined with kohl. It feels like someone has reached into my chest and squeezed the shit out of my heart and I have to stop staring at her, but I can't.

Not until I hear "There's my girl!" in Chase's affectionate voice and it's like someone's dumped a bucket of Gatorade over my head and drawn latte art with my internal organs.

Does that even make sense? I don't know. Nothing does.

I force myself down the stairs in my silver platform heels and take the hands he extends, accepting the kiss he drops delicately on my cheek so as not to mess up my makeup. With every move he makes you can tell he's done this before—been the handsome guy picking up his beautiful date who's told him not to muss anything before pictures. But that knowledge doesn't affect me and I don't know if it's because I'm aware of who he's dated in the past, or because I feel strangely numb as everything moves around me.

We pose for pictures—in a group of eight, in our quartet, in couples. I make a point not to watch Kiki and Jasmine take their photos, but when I sneak glances, it's clear that Kiki was telling the truth. Jasmine doesn't put her arms around Kiki the way Chase does to me, and they don't take classic shots of one of them gazing into the other's eyes, though maybe that's because they're the same height.

I don't know if Jasmine tells Kiki she looks beautiful the way Chase tells me I do, though Kiki definitely does look beautiful in her gothic gown with its corset bodice, and I'm jealous even though it's stupid. But there are a thousand pictures of me and Jasmine together from this past summer—selfies on the beach and pictures taken by Keisha at parties and portraits forced by Declan and Mom before events where our presences were requested. It feels like we should take one for them, at least. Except, of course, no one knows how closely our parents work together.

"Everything OK?" Chase murmurs, his hand warm through my thin dress, and I assure him that it is without even having to think about it.

It's Homecoming. I'm Chase Harding's date. How could it not be?

Everyone piles into the limo, and Chase immediately pulls me close. Part of me is happy to let him, and part of me wants to claw my way out and end this night before it even begins. I hate that I feel this way on a night that should be one of the best of my life, especially since I have a weirdly good chance of being named Homecoming Queen, but I hate so many things about how I feel lately. This is just one more on the pile.

"Time to open that champagne!" Lucas whoops, and suddenly there's foam everywhere and everyone's laughing and a bottle is being passed around. I don't want any, but that doesn't stop me from drinking when it comes my way, and it's so nice to have something occupying me that I take an extra sip. And then another. And another.

"Save some for the rest of us, Mrs. Harding!" Shannon yells, and everyone cracks up, even Chase. I try to smile, but the name makes me want to crawl out of my skin. Even Jasmine's laughing. How is Jasmine laughing?

I pass the bottle along and now I don't know what to do with my hands, so I take one of Chase's and twine my fingers with his. I know in my heart that he's warm and safe, but it's not translating, no matter how much I squeeze. Even when he kisses the top of my head.

"You excited to watch your boyfriend win Homecoming King?" Jasmine asks, and everyone else cheers while Chase hangs his head modestly.

"Are you kidding?" Apparently, Gia's had some champagne too. "This is literally Lara's dream come true. Like, *literally*."

I shoot daggers at her with my eyes, but she's completely oblivious, as is everyone else.

"Who knew so many years fangirling on the sidelines would pay off?" Shannon says innocently, and then giggles like she's had too much to drink, even though the bottle hasn't reached her yet. Gia and Jasmine join her, even though I know—I *know*—I never talked to Jasmine about that, which means Shannon has. How much time have they spent laughing at me behind my back? What kinds of friends do that?

Chase squeezes my hand and tells them to shut up and pass the champagne. He's trying to be kind, but I don't want it. I don't want any of this. I just want to climb through the sunroof and run home to my mom, leaving my stupid heels in the dirt.

Every glimpse I catch of Jasmine hurts my heart and feels like the worst betrayal, worse than Shannon, even, because she knew me in a way Shan never has, and because for everything I love about Shannon, I never expect more from her than this. She's there when I'm in need, when shit hits the fan. That's not nothing, but it isn't what I got from Jasmine. She doesn't open my eyes to different ways of looking at things. She doesn't make me feel like the best version of myself. She doesn't make me feel like I can do anything, like I don't just matter, but am in fact *significant*.

How did the girl who was once my biggest cheerleader become . . . this?

Chapter Eighteen

THEN

The seafood boil on the beach was such a success that Brea decided to have a smaller one for her birthday a couple of weeks later. I'm about to reply to our group text with a "Can't wait!" when Jasmine beats me to answering. *So sorry, Brea—going to my mom's that wknd.*

Immediately the chain floods with *boooo* and *we'll miss you!* But my fingers stay still. I'd never spent an evening out with everyone minus Jasmine. I'm not afraid I can't handle it—I'd definitely become friends with everyone in my own right—but . . . everything sounds like less fun without her there.

I open our private text thread, which is mostly full of *be there in 5* and *do you have my blue nail polish?* and start to tap out a message, but what do I even say? *I'll miss you* feels silly; I can say that on the group text like everyone else. *I didn't know you were going away for the weekend* is way too clingy.

While I'm thinking it over, a message pops up. For a second I panic that I'd written something without even realizing it, but no, this message from Jasmine is completely unprompted.

Jasmine: *Hey, I know this is really random, but if you're up for it, I could use a friend when I go see my mom this weekend.*

A follow-up: *no pressure*, followed by a nonsensical string of emojis.

The rush of certainty that yes, I do want to go with Jasmine to see her mom, hits like frappuccino-induced brain freeze. *Sure, sounds fun*, I write back.

Jasmine: *Just a warning*

Jasmine: *She's very into Shabbat dinner.*

Jasmine: *Hope you like lentil soup and tamarind in everything.*

Lara: *I have no idea what tamarind is, but if it's anything like crawfish, I can handle it.* I tack on a strong-arm emoji.

She sends back a laugh-cry one. *It's not. But you can handle it.*

I probably *can* handle tamarind, but meeting Sylvia Halabi is . . . a lot. In the very best way.

"Come in, come in," she ushers us, her voice as low and melodious as Jasmine's imitation of it. She gives Jasmine a big, dramatic kiss on each cheek, turns and does the same to me. "It's so nice to meet the famous Larissa!"

Famous, huh? The idea that Jasmine's mentioned me to her mom—more than once—makes me a little light-headed, even though obviously she had to in order to bring me. But maybe that feeling is from the Chanel that envelops Ms. Halabi like a summer breeze, softened only by my face being mashed into her silk blouse too tightly to smell much. "It's nice to meet the famous Jasmine's Mom," I manage, and she laughs, deep and throaty like her daughter.

"Such a pretty girl," she says affectionately, tugging one of my curls.

She's one to talk. Jasmine's mom is stunning, with the same thick, glossy black hair and liquid gold eyes as her daughter, which are even more striking against her deeper bronze skin. She's meticulously made up, and I worry we've interrupted her on her way out to something.

"No," Jasmine says, reading my mind. "She looks like that all the time." Sylvia looks puzzled, and Jasmine says, "She's not used to someone wearing a full face of makeup to have dinner with her daughter."

Embarrassed, I mumble, "You look great," and she laughs. She's much easier to make laugh than her daughter, but it's still hard not to be anxious against the backdrop of her neat, expensive perfection. The house is all marble and gold and glass, stunning and lavish in a very different way from Declan's. I could see how they'd been confused into thinking they were a match before realizing they were actually polar opposites.

"Let's go to the kitchen," she says, an arm around each of us, and we enter a white marble palace that smells so good I have to wipe my mouth to keep the drool at bay. There's a woman standing at the stove, stirring a pot, a long dyed-red braid skimming her waist. "This is Camella. I need a helper while my daughter's too busy swimming and tanning to help me stuff eggplant." Her voice is teasing, and she gives Jasmine a peck on the cheek.

Jasmine says hi and I introduce myself, and Camella gives us a quick smile and goes back to stirring.

Sylvia steers us back out. "Jasmine, why don't we give Larissa a tour of the house?" She doesn't even wait before leading me through each room, explaining every photograph, telling me the story behind each piece of artwork, and describing the purpose of every piece of Judaica. I'm proud to come in knowing a few, like mezuzahs and menorahs—my mom and I are technically Jewish too, though we're not remotely affiliated—and Sylvia seems similarly pleased about it.

We end with Jasmine's room, and Sylvia declares she's going to check on the food, leaving us standing in Jasmine's doorway. There are definitely some personal items in Jasmine's room at the beach house, but it's clear that this is where she *lives*. I sweep into the room to examine every inch of it.

"This vanity is amazing," I declare, walking over to the glass-and-mirror table immediately. It's covered in makeup and gorgeous perfume bottles, none of which I've ever known Jasmine to wear. In the Outer Banks, she smells like sunscreen and peach lotion and honeysuckle shampoo and chlorine and salt water. In Asheville, apparently, she smells like Dolce & Gabbana. "Since when do you wear perfume?"

"Since never." She cracks a smile as she collapses onto her huge, fluffy bed. "My mom doesn't think an outfit is complete without Chanel, so she keeps buying me fragrances in hopes I'll find my equivalent, but eh. It makes me feel old."

"Your mom looks like she's thirty."

"No wonder she likes you."

I continue snooping around, looking at pictures of Jasmine and her friends—Laila is easy to pick out—and family, brushing my fingers over her enormous collection of graphic novels, and riffling through her closet. "I cannot believe you have this much here given how much clothing you brought to the beach."

"What can I say? Halabi women like to shop! But we also give a lot to charity," she says, crossing her arms a little defensively.

"I don't doubt it." If there's one thing both Sylvia and Jasmine radiate, it's having a warm heart. "But wow, this is . . . impressive."

"SYs don't mess around. Wait until you see dinner."

She is not kidding. Sylvia calls us in a few minutes later, and my eyes widen when I realize how much there is. "Did your mom think *all* of your friends were coming?" I whisper to Jasmine.

"Oh, no. She went light for just the three of us."

Jasmine has got to be kidding. After we have wine and round, golden challah studded with seeds, enough food emerges from the kitchen to put the seafood boil to shame. As promised, there's an incredible lentil soup, and by the time I finish, I'm already half full. But the hits keep coming, and I find I can't say no—not to the football-shaped kibbeh stuffed with meat and pine nuts, nor to the mini pizza-looking things called lahmajun whose slightly sour taste Jasmine explains to me is the infamous tamarind, nor to the roast chicken spiced with cinnamon.

"I appreciate a girl with a healthy appetite," Sylvia says with a smile, and I blush. I don't usually eat that much, but the food is so good and Jasmine keeps encouraging me to "just taste" the stuffed onions and "have one bite" of the flaky bastel. I'd expected the food to be spicy, but it isn't at all, not in the hot sense. It's *flavorful*—more than anything else I've ever had in my life.

My mother would hate it.

"I told her you were a great cook," Jasmine says with no small amount of pride.

"She did." I take a gulp of water from my glass and notice Sylvia has barely eaten. Jasmine mentioned that too—her mother loves to cook far more than she loves to eat. I selfishly hope that means we'll be going back with leftovers.

Sylvia pats Jasmine's hand affectionately, and a wave of missing my mom comes over me. But it's quickly replaced by the realization that this is Jasmine's normal. I'm looking at the life she's coming back to after the summer—the food, the Friday night dinners, the vanity covered in perfume bottles. She won't be returning to New York with her dad, and none of us will be staying at the beach.

Suddenly, I'm not hungry anymore.

"So, you know I like to cook," Sylvia says to me. "Tell me, Larissa. What do you do for fun?"

"She's a writer," Jasmine says before I can get a word out, definitely knowing I wouldn't have said a word about it if she didn't force it. "She's been writing a book this summer."

My blush before was nothing compared to the heat level in my cheeks now. "It's nothing. It's for fun."

"Doesn't everything always start for fun?" Sylvia says with a shrug. "You know, my sister Rachel is a writer. A journalist. But she's been asked to consider turning her work into a book. If you ever want to talk to someone about publishing, I'm sure she'd be happy to speak with you."

It's the first time I've let "writer" be attached to my name, and it makes me itchy in a way that isn't as bad as it sounds to have someone take it seriously. I can't imagine talking to a professional about it, ever, but I say "maybe, thank you" through a mouthful of rice.

"Rachel's really cool," Jasmine tells me. "She does a ton of reporting on the Middle East and she's been *everywhere*. She wins awards and stuff."

"Where is she now?" I ask.

"Officially, she lives in DC, but barely. She's probably traveling somewhere like Morocco or Jordan." Jasmine says it a little dreamily, and it's obvious Rachel is kind of her idol.

It must be obvious to Sylvia too, because she says, "It's interesting how cool you find it when Rachel travels, considering you used to have a meltdown every time your father did when you were little. I used to beg him not to go because I couldn't take another one, but of course, that never stopped him."

Immediately, Jasmine stiffens. We've talked about how our moms do that thing where they find ways to mention our dads just to criticize them. But while I don't care—I know my dad's a dick and I have nothing to do with him—Declan is very much in Jasmine's life.

I don't know whether Sylvia realizes she's pissed off her daughter or senses that might've been a little much in front of company, but she gives an embarrassed cough, takes a sip of water, and asks what my father does.

I feel bad for both of them—for all of us, really. "Pays child support on time," I say, and there's a stunned silence before Sylvia bursts out in laughter. That even makes Jasmine grin.

"What more can we expect from them, really?" Sylvia says dryly, and we all laugh again.

It's a weird night.

In the best way.

We talk until the tall white candles Sylvia lit to bring in the Sabbath have melted to nothing and only traces of honey and pistachio crumbs remain on the dessert tray. Then we sip tea with real mint leaves in it while Sylvia shows me old photos of Jasmine, and I laugh at her extensive princess phase until there are actual tears in my eyes. By the time we go to bed, it's nearly midnight, and I feel like I'm glowing from the inside out from the warmth of it all.

There's a guest room, but there's no discussion of me

sleeping in it; Jasmine has as big a bed here as she does in the Outer Banks. We change into pajamas and brush our teeth and slide in together like I belong with her here as much as I do there.

I imagine these sheets still smelling like me when she comes back, even though they won't.

"Hey, thank you," I say softly, curling up in the mound of pillows on my side of the bed.

"For what?" Her voice is thick with sleep, her eyes already closed.

"For bringing me here to meet your mom. For Shabbat dinner." I inhale her sweet shampoo, the light trace of perfume that's been pressed into her skin from Sylvia's throughout the night. "For not laughing at me about the whole writing thing?"

"Why would I laugh at you?" she murmurs, halfway to dreamland. I feel fingers brush mine, intertwining, holding tight. "You're gonna do amazing things, Tinkerbell."

A few moments later, her soft snoring fills the air, and I let it lull me to sleep, her hand warm in mine.

Chapter Nineteen

NOW

The dance isn't much better than the limo ride, but it's easier to blend in with the crowd and get some space from the other girls. Chase is having a great time—that much is clear—and it's a little infectious. I do my best to let go of the digs and champagne headache and enjoy the night like I'm supposed to. When Chase kisses me, I kiss back. When he grinds against me on the dance floor, I press right back against him, feeling how badly he wants me. I smile for pictures, smile when people comment on how adorable his asking me to the dance was, smile when recent graduates come over to say hi and compliment him on his season, smile when Dee Harker, who was on the JV squad with me when I was a freshman and she was a sophomore, says, "I guess it's true that patience is a virtue!" and nods in his direction.

Even people who've graduated can't see me as

anything more than The Girl Who's Always Loved Chase Harding.

Onstage there's a tap at the mic and a screech of feedback. My stomach sinks. The time has come to announce Homecoming King and Queen. Even through all my dreams of standing alongside Chase in our crowns, I've never really believed that Homecoming Queen is a title I could win—not as long as Shannon's around. And that's fine; it's only a cheap plastic crown. But it was a fun dream . . . or it was until I realized it might be more than that. Judging by the amount of attention we're getting tonight, I might actually have a shot.

I don't think anyone has ever wanted a crown less.

They announce the court for the guys, and we cheer as Lucas, Chase, and a bunch of other guys jog to the stage. Immediately, the crowd starts chanting "Harding! Harding! Harding!" and Vice Principal Kanner smiles wryly and says, "Well, I guess your Homecoming King won't come as any surprise—Chase Harding!"

I don't know how to whistle, but I try, and I clap along with everyone as my boyfriend bends to accept his crown. It looks perfect on him, like it was always meant to sit on his head and bring out the sparkle in his eyes.

How would I look in the matching crown?

Would it look like it was made for me too?

I don't have to wait long to find out whether I'll be joining him. The more boring job of crowning one of the guys in near-identical tuxes is done, and it's time for the queens. They announce Shantay Reynolds and Christina Morse and, bam, there it is—"Larissa Bogdan!"

And, quieter but still audible, Shannon and Jasmine's whispered "Chase's girlfriend!" and peals of laughter that follow me all the way to the stage.

I'm seething as the rest of the names are called, including Shannon's, and I watch her sweetly preen like she didn't just mock her best friend as a pretender ten seconds earlier. For the first time in our lives, I want to beat her, want to yank this dream of hers she's acting like she never had all the way out from under her.

And then, I do.

"Your Homecoming Queen is . . . Larissa Bogdan!"

The room bursts into applause when my name is announced as the winner, and sure, maybe it's because I'm Chase's girlfriend, but I don't give a damn. I smile so brightly at the sound that I'm sure Jasmine can see it from wherever she is, and Shannon can't avoid it from her vantage point on the stage. I don't want them to miss a single clap as the crown is placed on my head, and I certainly don't want them to miss Chase sweeping me into a dramatic movie kiss as the entire room explodes.

"Congratulations, my queen," he murmurs with a smile. "As if there was any doubt."

"I believe it's time for us to dance, my king."

We head down to the dance floor and it feels like I should be wearing something dramatic and floor-sweeping rather than a sparkly full-skirted cocktail dress that barely clears my knees, but the way Chase looks at me when the spotlight finds us in the crowded gym makes it clear he thinks I look plenty regal. I try to focus all my attention on him, and while I succeed in ignoring the people snapping pics of us to post with crown emojis, I can't help searching for Jasmine in the crowd.

I want her to see this, how real it is, how real *we* are.

But when I find her, she's making vomiting motions at Kiki, who mercifully refuses to laugh.

Suddenly, I can't see Chase or the spotlight or anything else other than *red*.

How fucking *dare* she? What is her absolute need to make sure I'm miserable at all times? She *chose* to drop out of touch with me and send me back to my life without so much as a note that whoops, by the way, she'd be moving here and I'd have to see her every fucking day. What am I supposed to do with that? What am I supposed to do with *this*?

The minute the dance ends, I tell Chase I'll be right back. I have never appreciated more that he is not a follow-up–question kind of guy. He gives me a quick kiss and turns to his buddies, and I grab Jasmine by the wrist and yank her out into the hallway without giving a single damn who might be watching.

"What the hell, Lar—"

"No," I cut her off. "That is not your question. That is *my* question. What the hell happened to you, and why do you hate me?"

"God, Larissa, could you be any more dramatic?"

"Cut the shit, Jasmine. You've spent the entire last month acting like I barely exist, like last summer never happened. It happened. We spent every damn day together. Every damn *night* together. Did it all really mean so little to you?"

I expect a smartass answer, but she draws herself up to her full height, towering over me in her glittering stilettos. She's shaking, anger radiating off her skin. "You don't get to ask me that." Her voice drips with venom. "You don't get to tell me I'm the one who doesn't give a shit when you're the one practically married to someone else."

"God, I'm not—"

She throws up her arms, bangles jangling. "Yeah, you are, and that's fine. You have a life and so do I and neither of us has to explain or apologize."

"I'm not asking for an explanation or apology! I want *you* back! Where did *you* go?"

"I am right. Fucking. Here," she spits. "How do you not get that? I am here. In my senior year. Away from my friends, my life, my *mom*. Why do you think that is, Larissa?"

"How am I supposed to know when you won't tell me anything? When you didn't even tell me about your parents changing up custody? You knew you were coming to my school and you didn't even tell me!"

She looks like she wants to tear every meticulously styled strand of her thick black hair out of her head. "My parents didn't change up custody; *I* did. And I told you why. I fucking *sang* in front of everyone. In front of Shannon. In front of your boyfriend. I made a complete ass of myself, like I've been doing every single minute just by being here, and I still have to watch you with him tonight, and then you have the nerve to ask me—"

"You *sang*?" None of the rest of her words are clicking, and I have to close my eyes to shut them out. To flash back to the night her cruelty almost broke me. "You came all the way here to remind me to keep our summer a secret? You really didn't have to worry about that, Jasmine. Message received. I haven't told a soul, and you've made it plenty clear that it didn't mean a damn thing to you."

She blinks slowly. "Are you fucking kidding me?"

"None of this is a joke to me," I snap. "Apparently you don't feel the same way. Well, congratulations on making me feel like shit that night, same as you've been doing since you got here."

She buries her face in her hands, and I hear a muffled "fuck" through her fingers.

For the first time since before we got in the limo, I feel my anger slip a little, my guard dropping. Gently, I pry her hands away. "What am I missing here, Jas?"

"Everything," she says with a short laugh. "God, Larissa. Everything."

"Well, can you please fill me in? Because you're confusing me. As usual. Pardon me for not knowing how to interpret things." I scratch at the top of my dress, which suddenly feels itchy and way too tight.

"Okay, well, apparently I'm about to clear shit right up." She exhales sharply and folds her arms over her chest, which I think is a defensive move until I realize she's hugging herself. "The lyrics, Tinkerbell. Or rather, the lyric. You didn't hear it."

The lyric.

I was so focused on the song choice, on blocking out what I thought she was trying to say, that I missed the lyrics entirely. In a flash I know exactly which one she means.

Because I'm the one who introduced her to the magic of Demi Lovato when she finally let me take over the music in the Jeep.

I'm the one who taught her that very lyric.

I can picture it like it was ten minutes ago, the wind whipping our salt-sticky hair through the open windows on our drive back from the ferry as "Cool for the Summer" wound down through the speakers.

THEN

"She changed the lyrics of the song for her 2018 tour during Pride month to 'Go tell your mother.'" I drop a random fun fact I learned from Demi Lovato stans on Instagram.

"Huh," says Jasmine, tapping a finger on the wheel. "That's . . . definitely different."

"It is," I agree. "Just one word—'go' instead of 'don't'—and it made her fans so damn happy, I literally saw pictures of rainbow shrines."

"Well, makes sense. I mean, it's Pride month. 'Tell your mom about it' is certainly prouder than, like, 'hide your secret shame girl.'"

I snort. "'Secret shame girl' sounds like the title of really terrible porn."

"*You* sound like the title of really terrible porn," Jasmine retorts.

Like that, the conversation is over.

And the next night, in front of a bonfire, everything changes.

NOW

One look at Jasmine's face, wide open with heartbreak, and I know exactly which version she sang.

"I didn't sing that to you because I wanted you to forget the summer," she says softly, confirming. "I sang it to you because I wanted you to remember how good it was. And I know it was a stupid night to do it, but it felt like my last chance before I lost you for good. When I finally got the nerve to look at you, it was clear I'd already lost you before I even got here." Her gaze meets mine, and it looks like it takes all the effort in the world on her part. The least I can do is hold it.

"I moved in with my dad because I could not get you out of my fucking head. I thought about going back to school and pretending our summer was just a summer, and I couldn't do it. I thought that maybe if I came here, we'd have a chance to be something real, but I didn't know how to tell you I was coming. And before I could even see you, you had a boyfriend, and I was stuck here. Watching you live this perfect life that was already full without me. I've been trying to carve something out and save what's left of my dignity and my senior year, but I'm pretty sure I'm in love with you and I just need to go crawling back to my mom. My heart can't take you breaking it anymore."

Her gaze drops, but she doesn't walk away. "I'm sorry I've been an asshole all night. For longer than tonight, I guess. I really didn't handle it well that coming to Stratford wasn't what I hoped it would be."

"Because you hoped . . ." God, I feel slow. And yet my pulse is racing. "Jasmine. Why didn't you say anything? You had a billion chances!"

"Did I?" she says, and maybe I've been breaking her heart, but the sadness in her voice cracks mine wide open. "It feels like I never had one at all." She turns to walk away, and I don't know what to say, but I know I don't want her to go.

Then she turns back.

"Look, I should tell you—I'm bi. I was questioning it for a while, but when you came along this summer I felt like I finally knew for sure. And maybe for you, it was liking the taste of my cherry ChapStick or whatever. But even though this has all hurt like hell and honestly kind of sucks, it's good to know for sure who I am. So, thank you, I guess."

She sounds so certain. She's *been* certain, while I've been floating along, thinking we were both in the same weird and nameless territory of summer.

I don't know what to say.

I don't know what to think.

I don't know what I am.

And it doesn't matter, because she's gone.

Chapter Twenty

I don't go back into the dance. I can't see Chase now, can't prance around in a tiara, and I definitely can't see Jasmine. Luckily, when someone does surface to find me in the hallway, it isn't either of them—it's Kiki.

"You know," I say.

"I know."

"You always did, didn't you? How?"

Kiki taps her nose. "I have pretty excellent powers of deduction. Also, you stare at each other a *lot* when you think no one's watching. Like, a lot. And a few of the things you've each said about your summers line up, and that fire pit picture you texted us—Jasmine has a really similar one on Instagram. Finally, I looked up her dad. It wasn't hard from there."

"Kiki's on the case."

She smiles proudly. "Always." Her face turns serious. "Look, I know Chase has been the dream for literally ever, but . . . how do you feel? Unless you don't wanna talk about it."

Do I wanna talk about it?

How do I feel?

THEN

Carter's end-of-summer party is a lot like his beginning-of-summer party, which doesn't have anyone complaining. On the beach laughing and drinking and dancing and staring into the bonfire with everyone else, I know this is going to be the summer I think about a billion years from now. I can't believe I'm leaving tomorrow. I can't believe I won't be living steps away from the ocean anymore. I can't believe I'll never fall off Derek's Jet Skis again or get destroyed by Keisha and Carter at spades or have spa nights complete with Brea's sheet masks.

I can't believe this is it for me and Jasmine.

As much as I'll miss everyone, it's killing me that we're spending our last night with a billion other people. I keep trying to make eye contact with her, but every time I do, she's swept away by someone wanting her to play flip cup, or I'm yanked into a selfie by Owen or Brea. I keep wanting to drag her close, to imprint the feeling of her skin on mine, but I don't have any excuses. My mind can't come up with a single justification for why I need to grab her hand right now, or how to pull her away for a walk along the water, just the two of us.

We're all about the excuses, the setup, the ways we

happen to fall onto each other's mouths and hands. It's just what happens when you're hanging out alone and watching a movie, or swimming, or lying in the hammock together, or spreading out on the grass to watch the stars, or taking pictures of sunsets, or feeling lazy in a canoe.

It's just what happens for us over and over again and it's so good I can't stop thinking about it, wanting to kiss that spot on her neck, wanting to touch the incredibly soft skin on her shoulder blades, wanting to feel her hands tracing my hipbone on a path to making me see stars.

How can I not have an excuse for our last night?

Watching her flirt with Carter certainly isn't helping any, so I decide to give myself a little breathing room and take that walk on the beach myself. I have my phone to keep me company, and I scroll through pictures hoping the sight of Gia smiling hugely from a pyramid at cheer camp or Shannon posting a picture with yet another cute Parisian guy will get me excited enough about what I'm going back to that I'll stop being sad about what I'm leaving behind.

But it's Kiki's latest post that stops me. She's been working on her lettering, writing cheesy quotes in funky fonts and posting them to Instagram. Her newest is "Seize the Day," written in swirly hot pink gothic letters, and it's such an un-Kiki quote that it makes me laugh.

I'm still laughing when I take its completely cliché advice and retrace my steps on the beach right back to the party, to Jasmine, and whisper in her ear.

"Look, I don't have a clever way to say this, but it's my last night, so I'm going to set the bullshit aside. The only thing I want to do tonight is go back to your house and take our clothes off. Can I say that?"

For the longest minute in the world, I brace myself for a literal or metaphorical slap in the face, or worse. The words came out easily enough, but my entire body is trembling. Then she squeezes my hand and like magic it stops, long enough for me to make my rounds hugging and kissing everyone goodbye when Jasmine announces that we're heading back. I make promises to text and otherwise keep in touch but I barely even know what I'm saying because I've just flat-out told a girl I want to have sex with her and we're on our way to do that and I feel like I'm gonna burst into flames.

We don't say a word on our way back. We don't say a word when we crash into each other the second we make it inside the house, kissing so furiously I expect one of us to draw blood. There's no talking as we pull at each other's clothing and fall onto her bed, shutting and locking the door behind us.

There's no talking, but it isn't silent either. For the first time, I don't waste precious energy holding in every desperate sound that rises into my throat at the scrape of her nails on my skin. I make no effort to hold still against the way her teeth have me writhing on the sheets. This is the most in the moment I have ever been, and with every gasp of air I'm grateful for the scrap of honesty that got us here.

Beyond that, I'm not doing any thinking.

Her breathing goes fast and shallow as I kiss and

touch down her body to her hip bones, and look up for an okay for more even though I'm not a hundred percent sure that *I'm* okay. Her nodding is fast and furious but it's the sight of her hands grasping the sheets with white-knuckled fists in anticipation that halts any hesitation I might've had at venturing into new territory.

It isn't silent, not when she cries out minutes later, and not when our bodies find new ways to fit and rock together, and not when we grasp each other so tightly we leave claw marks in each other's skin. Every time I think we can't get any closer, I learn I'm wildly underestimating us. We spend so many tangled and sweaty hours exploring each other that I'm not even sure at what point I finally pass out.

It takes a second for the night to come rushing back, for me to remember why I'm completely naked in Jasmine's bed and clutching a sheet around myself. I spent last night having sex—so much sex, *incredible* sex—with a girl. A girl I'm leaving behind today when my mom and I fly back to New York.

A girl I might never see again.

A girl who might've left *me* behind first.

Then I hear the clanging of pans out in the kitchen, and I'm filled with mixed emotions as I think about seeing Jasmine again after last night. But I only have a few hours left, and I still need to pack, so I'll take being uncomfortable if it means I'm not missing my chance to say goodbye entirely.

I rummage around on the floor for my bra and

underwear and grab shorts and a T-shirt from Jasmine's drawers—I've certainly spent enough of this summer lifting her clothing. But I still think *oh, shit* when I walk out of her room and see she's not alone in the kitchen—Declan's with her, sipping from a mug of coffee.

"Larissa! I thought you'd be packing."

I don't even know what to say. Jasmine and I have had plenty of sleepovers this summer but for some reason I am convinced he can tell I slept with his daughter last night in a very, very different way. I will my tongue to unstick itself but can't seem to get a single word out.

"We wanted to hang out after the party, and Larissa fell asleep. I couldn't, so I let her have the bed and passed out watching a movie on the couch," Jasmine explains, pushing scrambled eggs around a skillet. "These are just about done, Dad."

There's no invitation for me to stay, and I really do have to pack, so I say my goodbyes and a lukewarm thank-you to Jasmine for letting me stay over.

We don't talk when we hug goodbye.

It is, in fact, silent.

Later, at the airport, she texts me a single heart emoji. I text her one back.

It's the last we ever speak until she shows up at Stratford High.

NOW

Do I wanna talk about it?

How do I feel?

"She thinks she's in love with me."

Kiki smiles without any trace of sarcasm. It's weird and I don't think I've ever seen that on Kiki's face and I'm not sure what to do with it. "How'd hearing that feel?"

The first word that comes to mind is *confusing*. I didn't think love was in the equation. I didn't think feelings were even an *option*. I don't know what being in love means to her, and I definitely don't know what it means to me. I thought I was in love with Chase all those years, but that wasn't this. That made me feel feverish and ridiculous and like I wanted to follow him everywhere, to have done all these things with him.

But now I've done so many of those things, and it feels like what I did was check off a list.

With Jasmine, I don't have a list. And I don't want to follow her anywhere; I want to go everywhere together. I want to do things *with* her. I want us to *make* that list.

My feelings for her are so different from what I thought love was, but does that mean it's not love? Does that mean it *is* love?

"God, I don't know."

Kiki tugs one of my curls. "I may not have any relationship experience, but I'm pretty sure that's okay. It is for tonight, at least. Look—you're Homecoming queen, and ditching Chase would be kinda public and humiliating. I don't think you're really looking to do that."

"Definitely not," I say quickly, my stomach sinking at the thought. "Chase has been amazing, and he's having such a good time."

"Well, you deserve that too. Jasmine is already

gone—she called an Uber. So, here's what I think. Let's finish out the night. Let's go have fun. No big decisions, no deciding your romantic future, no stress. Just dancing and drinking and having one last big high school night. Tomorrow, you can deal. What do you think?"

I think . . . it feels like finally taking a breath. "I'm in."

"Well, that is delightful," says Kiki, linking her arm through mine, "because I am currently down a date and I could use the company."

Chapter Twenty-One

"Dealing" starts earlier than I expect it to, because when my mom wakes me up with a dish of pickled cucumbers—her surefire hangover cure—I know I'm in trouble. "Enough sleeping. Eat, Dotchka," she says, holding it close enough to my nose to make me gag.

"Mama—"

"Don't 'Mama' me when you are still passed out at two in the afternoon the day after a dance at which there isn't supposed to be any drinking. Now eat."

I hate to admit it, but they work. "Did you really think there wasn't going to be any drinking at Homecoming? Besides, none of us were driving—the limo brought me home."

"At what time?"

I mumble "3:00 a.m." as quietly as I can, but she catches it anyway.

"Three?! Bozhe moi. Lara. There's a reason you have a curfew, and I think it's a pretty generous one—"

"If you wanted me to take the limo and stay safe with my friends, I couldn't come home until everyone else was," I point out. In truth, I have no memory of what we were doing until that time, but judging by the gross, fuzzy taste in my mouth, it involved a lot of vodka. "Anyway, I'm home. Safe. And eating pickled cucumbers." I take another one, as if it'll make the argument for me.

She raises one of her eyebrows. "I take it you had fun."

Did I have fun? I know I did all the things that are supposed to be fun. I danced and played drinking games and took a thousand pictures in my tiara.

I also know I avoided fooling around with Chase as much as possible and spent most of the night thinking about Jasmine until I drank enough to stop thinking about anything at all.

"I won queen," I say instead of answering her question.

"And was that fun?" she asks, because my mother is very smart.

I hug my covers to myself. I want to tell my mom the truth. I want to tell her about Jasmine and how confused I am, and I want her to stroke my hair and call me Larotchka and tell me everything is gonna be okay and to just listen to my heart.

I want to, but I am fucking terrified.

"Of course," I lie.

My mother always knows when anything less than the truth is falling from my lips; it's why I have to text if I'm being slightly dishonest about where I'm gonna be. My face shows everything. And I wonder what it's showing that's making her give me that "Oh, honey" look.

But she doesn't say anything. Just takes my hand.

And I fall apart.

My mother holds me while I cry into her shoulder, not moving even when I'm definitely getting snot all over her shirt. The hair stroking I'd been hoping for happens like clockwork, and I know that I'm running the risk of feeling it for the last time.

I can't bear that.

My mother is pretty literally my everything. It's why I barely complained about going to North Carolina for the summer. It's why I didn't argue with my father about me going to a state school. It's why I've never fought her having full custody.

It's why I have to tell her the truth, even though the very thought sends me into another round of tears.

"Larotchka, what happened? Did he hurt you?"

That's enough to make me pick up my head and wipe my nose. "No, God. No. Chase was great. Chase is always great. It's me. I'm a mess."

"You're not a mess; you're my wonderful daughter who is not fully escaping punishment for missing curfew, but that's beside the point for now." She gently wipes a tear from my cheek with a neatly manicured fingernail. "What's going on?"

I take a deep breath, and another, until I can talk without breaking into sobs. "I need to tell you something, but I don't want you to hate me."

She looks like I've slapped her, which makes me feel

worse. "You are my *daughter*. You are my whole heart, Larotchka. I could never." She squeezes my hands so hard it's like she's trying to push that fact into my skin.

"I . . . there's someone. Not Chase. Not . . . not a boy." I exhale slowly. "I met a girl. She's not my girlfriend or anything, but I think . . . I think that I want her to be. And I think she wants that too. And I know we've never talked about anything like this, but I didn't—"

Her fierce hug cuts me off and sets off a fresh round of tears, her whispered "Larotchka" ruffling my mess of curls. "Bozhe moi, you had me so worried. This— happiness—is a *good* thing. Someone who loves you is what I *want* for my daughter."

I didn't think I could clutch my mother any tighter, but I'm pretty sure I'm leaving claw marks in her back. "You've always told me how traditional baba Mila and deda Tolya are, how mad they were when you had me without marrying Dad. I didn't know how much tradi-tion was in you too."

"Do I seem traditional, Dotchka?"

"Well, there's a dish of pickled cucumbers in my bed, so, yes?"

She laughs gently, releases me, tucks one of my messy curls behind my ear. "Some things about Russia, they stick. Their laws on gay people, not so much. But I have to admit I am surprised after so many years of hearing about the legend of Chase Harding."

The mere mention of Chase, the knowledge that I have to tell him, makes me want to be sick all over again in a way Mama's top remedy can't cure. "It wasn't a lie,"

I assure her. "I'm not gay. I'm not sure what I am. I just know that this one girl makes me feel . . . everything. The rest, I'll have to figure out."

"You have plenty of time for that." She drops a kiss on the top of my head. "How about we have a girls' day? I'll get some ice cream and we can watch movies and put on those ridiculous face masks."

God, that sounds good. "Yes. Please. But I have to do something first." There's no point in putting off telling Chase. Whatever happens with Jasmine, he deserves to spend his senior year of superstardom with a girl who'll appreciate him. And I'm no longer that girl. "I'll come back right after, okay?"

She nods, knowing exactly where I'm going. "I'm proud of you, Lara."

"I'm pretty proud of me too," I say honestly, "even if this feels kind of horrible." I get up to get ready, turning away, and something hits me.

She hasn't asked about the girl.

She didn't say we'd watch movies while I tell her all about the person who's stolen my heart. She didn't ask who could've possibly made me forget about Chase Harding. Is that her way of giving me privacy? Or is this her way of keeping it—the truth of me—at a distance?

I want to say something, but I can't. I don't know if Jasmine told her parents the real reason she wanted to spend the year with Declan. What if she didn't? I can't put my mom in the position of keeping this secret from her dad, and I'm sure as hell not gonna be the one who outs Jasmine either. What if—

"He feels the same way I do, in case you're wondering," Mama says softly to my back. "He and Sylvia both do."

I turn slowly back around. "You knew."

She shakes her head. "Not exactly. I knew there was something special between you. I saw the way you were together. I saw you turn into a happier, more confident person around her. You wear your love for each other plain as day. I just didn't know what kind of love. Now I do."

"But you talked about it with Declan. And he talked about it with Sylvia."

"Sylvia was the one who first mentioned it, actually, after that weekend you spent at her house. She said she'd never seen Jasmine glow like that. And when Jasmine asked to spend the year here . . . there's a reason they gave in easily. I thought maybe it was only on her side, especially after all those years of your crush on Chase, but I see the glow on you too." She smiles. "It's beautiful. You're lucky to have each other."

"We don't yet," I tell her. "But we will. I hope. I don't know as what. But we'll figure it out."

"Yes, you will. Deep breaths, Larotchka. You will get through this."

I give her a kiss on the cheek, and then I'm off from one scary conversation to the next.

It doesn't occur to me until I'm ringing Chase's doorbell that I should've given him a heads-up. No matter—he's the one who answers the door, and he looks unfairly hot in a clingy T-shirt and shorts. For a brief second, I contemplate not going through with this. It would be so easy to keep riding the high of superstardom on Chase's arm, to keep spending time with this good-looking and charming boy who genuinely likes me. It's not like Jasmine would tell anyone; she can disappear back to Asheville and I can finish out this perfect year I've been having. I can wear my Homecoming crown and cheer at Chase's games and hold his hand at the movies and pose with him for pictures at prom. I don't have to blow that all apart.

Except I do. Because when I think about spending those Friday nights watching movies with Jasmine, when I think about Jasmine's hips beneath my fingertips when we dance, when I think about ice cream dates and road trips and planning for college and making out in the backseat of a car . . . she's the person I wanna do all that with.

She's my top-of-high-school-bucket-list prom date.

It's that simple, even if it isn't simple at all.

"Hey! I was just thinking about you." He drops a kiss on my cheek and steps aside to let me in. "I had a great time last night."

Well, that's gonna make this harder. "I'm glad, but I really need to talk to you about something."

"Oookay." He closes the door behind me and leads me into his living room. "You want a drink?"

"No, thank you. Can—can we just sit?"

"This sounds serious." He frowns. "This sounds breakup serious. Are you breaking up with me?"

I hesitate, because that's really not how I wanted to start this conversation, and anger flashes in his eyes. "Did you seriously hook up with me to become Homecoming queen and then dump me? That's really fucked-up."

"No," I assure him firmly. "God, no, Chase. It's not like that."

"Then what's it like?" he asks, his voice dipped in acid.

Deep breath. He's hurt. He's allowed to be hurt. "This isn't about Homecoming. You of all people *know* that I liked you forever. It's that . . . there was someone else, and I didn't really realize it until last night."

"Hold up. You *cheated* on me?"

"No!" God, I should've prepared this better. I scrub my face with my hands and groan. "I'm sorry; I am doing this really poorly. Let me start over." Another deep breath. "There was someone before you, and I didn't understand my feelings, and you came along, and— you're *Chase*. I have had a crush on you since I was in Little League with Kira and you were her string bean of a brother sitting on the sidelines. When you were interested in me, it kind of obliterated everything else. It helped me stop thinking about this thing I didn't wanna think about. But I couldn't stop thinking about it."

He scratches the back of his head. "Lara, I gotta be honest—I don't understand what you're talking about."

Aaaand I'm officially out of ways to dance around this. *Deep breath.* "It's a girl, Chase. I like a girl. I was with a girl this past summer."

"Uh . . . whoa." For the first time since he realized

this was the end of our relationship, he doesn't look mad. He looks stunned. As stunned as I feel that the words just came out of my mouth.

"That's exactly how I felt. I was so confused, and then you were into me, and I have liked you for *so long*. I thought if I had you, I could put her behind me. I *wanted* to put her behind me, to be with you. But it didn't work."

"I mean, this is the bisexual thing, right?" he says, and his voice does not sound kind. "Not being able to choose?"

I recoil as if Chase has slapped me, which it kind of feels like he has. "If by 'thing' you mean 'stereotype,' then yeah, it is. But this isn't that. I wanted you, Chase. For fucking *years*, I wanted you. You know it. Everyone at Stratford knows it. You had years to see something in me. But you didn't; someone else did. And I didn't know I was—" I snap off. I don't know how to say this without sounding stupid, without feeling stupid, without telling Chase too much.

"You didn't know you were what?" he asks, and I don't know how to read his voice anymore. It isn't mad or tired or sad, but I feel all of it in those six words. "Bi?"

And because that's not it—because that's only a tiny piece, and because I haven't been able to take the time to decide whether it's *my* piece—I say what I have to say. "I didn't know I was allowed to like her like that," I finish quietly. "I didn't know it was okay. I didn't know it could be more than 'girls just messing around' or 'girls having fun.' I had liked you—*really* liked you—for so long, I knew I wasn't gay. I knew I liked boys. And I knew *she* liked boys. And sometimes when you like the gender you're 'supposed' to like, it's not so clear what's happening with the others."

He furrows his brow in confusion. "But it's not like you don't know what bisexuality is. You have bi friends."

"Yeah, and the fact that it didn't look the same for them made it even more confusing. Jamie? Has been out forever. Kenny Cho? Announced that Evan Sanders was his boyfriend when we were literally standing in a sand-box, and then a week later he said Julie Morrow was his girlfriend now. I never had feelings like that for any girls until this summer. And my best friends are pretty much the hottest girls in school, so, you know—I'd have known."

That at least gets a tiny snort of a laugh from Chase, but then his face grows serious. "So, you really like her?"

"I really do."

"But you liked me too."

"I really did," I say, putting a hand on his arm. I hope he can tell how much I mean it. "If I'd known what was going on between me and her wasn't just a fling, I would've made different choices. I promise you that. I wasn't trying to string you along, Chase. Dating you was all of my dreams coming true. But I hadn't let myself re-alize that my dreams had changed."

He huffs out a breath. "I really, really want to be mad at you."

"You can be," I assure him. "The fact that I was gen-uine doesn't mean it doesn't feel like shit. And it's not like I don't feel shitty about it. I'd kill for no one to have gotten hurt in this scenario."

"I know you would," he says softly. "You're a good person, Lara. It's why I really, really fucking like you."

Present tense, still. And I guess in a way, it's present tense, still, for me too. But it isn't the way I feel about Jasmine. It's like the tail end of a romantic comet that's about to fizzle into something that isn't dazzling in the same way, but is more permanent, still stellar. "I would really, really like to stay friends," I reply. "When you're ready."

He nods. "Not yet. But someday. Maybe you'll come to one of my college games."

"I'd like that," I say, and I mean it. "I just need to spend a little more time on my face paint skills."

He gives me the tiniest trace of a smile, and I tuck it away to remember us by because I have no idea what it'll be like to see him in school on Monday. Things aren't gonna go neatly when his friends, my friends, and everyone else find out that not only did the Homecoming queen dump the king right after the dance, but she did it for another girl.

I'm probably in for day after day of hell.

And somehow, that feels better than when I was supposed to be in for day after day of heaven, and it felt like nothing at all.

We exchange quiet goodbyes, and my first thought is that I should head straight to Jasmine's, but the truth is, I'm not ready. The reality of Chase Harding might not have been what I wanted it to be, but this is still the end of a dream. I need to mourn it.

And the only person I wanna do that with is waiting

for me at home with tubs of ice cream, bright-green sheet masks, and every single rom-com Netflix has to offer.

Four hours, two movies, a thousand calories, and much glowing skin later, my mom makes what I suppose is an inevitable suggestion. "Why don't you invite your friends over for the next one? I'll order from Bamboo House and I think we have a few more of these sheet masks lying around." She gives my hand a quick squeeze. "I think you'll be happy to have them to talk to instead of just your old mama."

The thing is? I really want to.

The thing is? I'm really scared to.

The thing is? I think I need to. And if my mom is offering Bamboo House, I know she thinks I do too, because that's a special occasion place for us, and I guess in a way that's what this is.

"Okay," I say, my voice a wimpy whisper as I grab my phone and open our endless text chain to type out an invite that contains exactly no information other than that there'll be a movie and Chinese food.

I expect I'll get at least one of them replying that she's too hung over to make it out, but apparently chicken lo mein is exactly what they all require for recovery, because half an hour later, the three of them are standing at my door.

The second I see their faces, I crack. "Chase and I broke up."

Silence.

Then finally, Kiki says, "Holy shit."

Gia immediately sweeps me into a hug, and I know she thinks he dumped me, but I let her do it anyway, let them usher me inside and onto the couch. My mom is out picking up the food, and their attention is on me, waiting for me to pour out my heart. It takes me a minute to figure out what to say, and Gia takes the opportunity to jump right in. "Do we hate him?" she asks.

I laugh and squeeze her hand. "No, we don't hate him. He's great. It turns out I'm just . . . not his fangirl anymore."

Shannon's eyebrows shoot to the sky. "Wait. *You* broke up with *him*?"

It's hard not to exchange glances with Kiki, but I know if I do, Shan will pick up on it immediately and demand the truth. And while I finally feel safe figuring out my shit with them, I don't know what to say until Jasmine and I figure out where we go from here. "I did. I . . . realized I'm looking for something else."

"Wow." Shannon looks at me—really looks at me—and the corner of her mouth curls into the tiniest hint of a smile. "You really did change this summer."

My mom lets herself in then, the sound of the door saving me from having to respond. I jump up and take the bags from her hands, giving her a peck on the cheek and scurrying into the kitchen. I'm pulling out the takeout containers when I hear footsteps and see that Shannon has followed me.

"I'll be out in a second," I tell her, searching the cabinets for paper plates.

"I know." She glances into the living room, where my

mom is chatting with Kiki and Gia, and turns back to me. "Look . . . I'm sorry I was kind of shitty, telling Jasmine and everything. That wasn't cool."

Thank God there's nothing in my hands but plastic cutlery, because at the sound of Shannon Salter saying the word "sorry," forks and spoons go clattering to the countertop. "Did you just *apologize*?"

"It happens occasionally."

"It doesn't, though. We've been friends for more than ten years and I don't think it ever has."

"Okay, well, shut up, because I'm making it good."

I shut up. How can I not?

"I thought . . . I thought you were gonna disappear on me, okay?"

"For Chase?"

She crosses her arms. "Of course for Chase. You finally got the guy, Lara. You weren't gonna need my fashion advice or makeup tips or even car rides. I don't know what happened between the two of you, but he was smitten as fuck. Any idiot could see it. And, well, *every* idiot knows you were smitten with him, so."

I can't even believe what I'm hearing. Never in my life would I have imagined Shannon Marie Salter to have an insecure bone in her entire perfect body. "You really thought I would ditch you for a guy? After everything?"

"Chase wasn't just *a* guy, Lar. He's *the* guy."

"Okay, but you're *the* Shannon," I counter, raking a hand through my short blond curls. "I barely leave the house without you. I will *always* need you, and not for your clothing or makeup."

She picks up the cutlery, opens the cabinet I'd been reaching for, and pulls out the plates. "That used to be true, but things have changed. You seemed like you didn't need me anymore, and then I met Jasmine in AP French, and she seemed like she might, so."

"Shan, you will always be of the utmost importance. You are the person who got me over being embarrassed to buy tampons in public. You've been getting my ass to school on time since the day you got your license. When I got that horrifying zit right before picture day sophomore year, you spent like an hour making sure I didn't look like a human pizza. But there's more to being friends than being needed. You don't need to, like, provide a service, okay? Well, other than eyeliner application. I'm really reliant on that."

"Deal," she says, her lips curving at the corners.

I grab a bottle of Diet Coke from the fridge and bump it closed with my hip. "You were really straight-up trying to replace me, huh?"

"It sounds so bitchy when you put it that way."

"Yeah, because it *was* bitchy, Shan. That's why you're apologizing, remember?"

She sighs heavily. "Fine. Yes. It was bitchy. *I* was bitchy. But for what it's worth, Jasmine's cool. I think you'd really like her."

It's just . . . too much. I have to put down the soda. I have to put down everything because I have started cracking up and I feel like I will never stop. It's so loud that Gia and Kiki come rushing in to see what they're missing.

"What the hell?" Kiki looks back and forth between

me, who's laughing her ass off, and Shannon, who's looking at me like I am deranged.

When I finally manage to gather myself, I look Kiki right in the eyes and say, "Shannon thinks I would like Jasmine if only I got to know her."

"Oh." Kiki bites her lip so hard to keep from laughing that I think she's going to draw blood, and I lose it all over again.

"What the hell is going on here?" Gia asks Shannon, who just shakes her head.

Having sort of come out twice today so far, I know that when an opportunity arises, you have to take it. The laughter stops, and I do glance at Kiki this time. She gives me an encouraging look.

Deep breaths.

"I do like Jasmine. A little too much. It's, uh, kind of why I broke up with Chase."

For the second time in a minute, there's the familiar sound of plasticware clattering as Shannon drops it and the plates to the floor.

And then it's silent.

I turn to Kiki. "Uh, is this how it went when you told them you were going to prom with Jasmine?"

"No, but apparently they'd both already assumed I was gay."

"Aren't you?" Gia asks, her face screwed up in confusion.

Kiki laughs. Which absolutely does not mean she isn't. Or that she is.

"Okay, wait, back to Bogdan," Shannon demands. "So, the Chase obsession is over."

"Yes."

"But . . . Jasmine? *When?* I've never even seen you spend time together."

I fix my gaze on one of the takeout cartons, opening and closing the little tabs. "It's, uh, complicated?"

"It's not that complicated," Kiki says with a snort. "Jasmine's dad is Anya's boss. Jasmine's the girl Lara lived with all summer. God, do you guys *ever* listen to my podcast? You would be so much better at detective work if you did."

"Nicely done, Kiki," my mom calls from the living room, where she's apparently been listening to this entire conversation.

"Why, thank you," Kiki calls back.

Facepalm.

"So, you guys have been a couple this whole time?" Shannon asks.

"Of course not. No. I was very much with Chase until a few hours ago. And I'm not with Jasmine," I add quickly, partly because I'm not and partly because I don't know if going to prom on Kiki's arm counts as outing herself, but I'm certainly not doing it for her. "I just . . . have feelings. Of the confusing and complicated and definitely shouldn't be dating someone else while I have them variety."

Gia nods. "Got it. I think."

I turn to Shannon. "And you? Still mad? Less mad? More mad?"

She blinks and it seems to take forever, long enough that I'm afraid she's going to walk right out of my house and leave us with an extra portion of dumplings. Especially when her mouth twists into a frown.

And then she opens her mouth.

"Okay, I feel like I'm falling behind on coolness by not being into girls now. This may have been a very missed opportunity in Paris. I still have time to catch up in college, right?" She looks from me to Kiki, like we're somehow gurus in the Art of the Gay. "I mean, art girls are all free and into expression and whatever, right? Wasn't Frida Kahlo bi?"

I gawk at her.

"What?" she asks innocently, gathering the plates and cutlery back up.

"How did this become about you?"

"Isn't everything?"

"Not this," I snap. "Jesus, Shannon. Sexuality isn't something you buy in a Parisian boutique and wear for a season. This is kind of a big deal for me."

She blinks. Nods. "I'm being an asshole again."

"Yes," Kiki, I, and even Gia say at once.

"Points for self-awareness and saying 'I'm sorry' way faster this time?" she asks meekly.

I wrap my arm around her shoulders and kiss the top of her head. "I'm glad to have you back, Shan," I murmur.

"God, you are so sappy." But before we pile into the living room, laden with takeout cartons and soda, she gives me a quick squeeze.

Chapter Twenty-Two

It seems almost cruel that the morning after my own romance ended is the one in which I finally get to meet Clementine Walker face-to-face.

"I'm a huge fan," I tell her when Beth brings her to the café counter, wiping my hand on my apron before shaking hers. "I've read every single one of your books. Repeatedly."

"Well, that's always a nice thing to hear!" She has a big smile, bright teeth, and long blond hair that's clearly out of a bottle, but in a way that looks really cool with dark roots. It somehow makes me even more nervous that she's extremely nice, and everything else I'd thought to say to her flies out of my head.

I excuse myself to make her a coffee, and she even compliments the half-formed heart drawn in the foam. "It feels more complex that way," she assures me. "Like this is a heart that has been through some stuff."

"You have no idea," I mutter, grateful when Beth

calls for me to come get the cart of books for the signing.

The crowd starts trickling in about ten minutes before the event. I guess romance is a hotter genre in the Stratford area than I knew, because soon every seat in the store is full, and Beth's sending me to get more folding chairs. I barely get back to my spot at the café counter before Beth makes the grand introduction and everyone claps for Clementine.

"Thank you for coming," Clementine says, and she sounds so professional that it makes me want to be her all the more. She's pretty, she's confident, she's talented, and the huge rock on her left hand suggests she's got all her romantic shit figured out. I know from her posts on social media that she's got a hot husband and two adorable kids, and I bet she's never had her heart twisted up by a girl she'd become too afraid to call.

Thirty-six hours later, I still haven't spoken to Jasmine. I can't. I'm back to feeling like it was all in my head, like I've gone ahead and come out to my friends, and for what? What if she's changed her mind since the night of the dance? What if she's mad I didn't go after her? What if she thinks I'm still with Chase?

Part of me is so angry we didn't have this conversation back when we were exchanging heart emojis, letting a tiny little picture in a text thread mask everything we had to say to each other, everything we felt. I wouldn't have had to hurt Chase; I wouldn't have had to keep secrets from everyone . . .

But, if that hadn't all happened, would I ever have been able to get here?

And where exactly is here, anyway?

I just want to see her. When she'd first mentioned coming to this event, I was horrified at the thought of her showing up, but . . . I can't help wishing she had. These books were something I'd shared with her, something she knew mattered deeply to me. Hell, these books were directly responsible for making sure that night by the bonfire wasn't a one-time thing.

I really want to share this with her.

There's more applause, and I realize Clementine's done with her reading, and I quickly join in the clapping. After, Beth takes questions, and I force myself to clear my head and listen, knowing I'll regret it if I miss out on her wisdom.

"Where does the inspiration for your work come from?" asks a woman in a green sweater, twisting a long strand of pearls around her fingers.

"Pretty much everywhere," Clementine says with a smile. "This story in particular was inspired by a similar mishap on one of my vacations. Another woman took my suitcase by accident, and it made me wonder what it would be like to stumble into someone else's life when you're most in need of a change. Everything kind of spun off from there."

Green Sweater looks satisfied, and Beth takes the mic from her and hands it to a woman in a sleeveless denim shirt whose chunky rings flash in the light.

"How does your husband feel about you writing romance, specifically explicit sex scenes? Not that I'm complaining."

"Well, neither is he," Clementine says with a wink, and everyone laughs and applauds.

That's when I hear it—the familiar jingle of bangle bracelets. I crane my neck and sure enough, there's Jasmine, casual and beautiful in a soft pink sweater and jeans, her dark waves cascading over her shoulders.

She's here.

She's here without knowing how I feel. She's here without knowing if I'm still with Chase. She's here without knowing if I want to be friends or girlfriends or kick her out of my life completely. She's here and she's beautiful and she's so fucking brave, braver than I've ever been.

My hand flies into the air.

"Yes! The barista!" Clementine Walker says. "You have a question?"

"I do." My voice is shaking so badly and it's awful and embarrassing and forces me to take a deep breath as the whole room turns their eyes on me while Beth brings me the mic. "Do you ever . . . I mean, have you ever . . ." Another breath, and this time, I meet Jasmine's quizzical gaze, watch the way her teeth gently tug at her lip, and I steady. "Has the love interest ever turned out to be someone other than who you originally planned? Because I'm writing a book, and I had this great couple all planned out, but I can't seem to get my main character as interested in him as she is in her roommate."

Clementine smiles knowingly. "That's the thing about characters—you think you're in control, but even though they're fictional people, they tend to have their own minds. I think of it as the most amazing blessing when my characters tell me what they want, even if it involves a whole lot more editing than I planned! Did you know in *The One That I Haunt*, Zach's brother Tate was actually supposed to be the love interest? But once I realized that Zach and Angie's bond over their cats was going to be an unbreakable one, I changed paths, even though I was halfway through the draft and two weeks away from deadline."

There are gasps, and you just know they're all from empathetic writers.

"I know, right?" says Clementine, and she's chuckling as she wipes her forehead in a mock show of cleaning the sweat off her brow. "I can't believe I did it either. But just because you're telling a good story doesn't mean it's the *right* story. And I think it's really important to tell the right story." She looks right at me and answers so brightly that it's clear she can't tell my world happens to be turning upside down at that moment. "It sounds to me like the roommate is a relationship worth exploring."

"Yeah," I say slowly, picking out Jasmine in the crowd. "I'm pretty sure the roommate is my story."

I offer her a slight smile.

She offers one back.

And then we wait.

The event I'd been anticipating for weeks suddenly feels interminable, and when it's done, Jasmine takes her time making her way over, looking almost scared of what she'll encounter when she finally reaches the counter. "You're writing again," she says by way of greeting.

"I am. I got inspired, I guess."

Her smile is quick, and then she's playing with her fingers in a nervous way I've never seen from her. "Listen, Lara, I'm sorry for springing all of that on you at Homecoming. That wasn't the right way to talk about . . . any of this. I can't blame you for not reaching out afterward."

"I couldn't," I tell her.

She casts her eyes down. "I know."

"I was busy."

She nods.

"I had to tell my mom I'm crazy about a girl. I had to break up with Chase. I had to tell my friends. It's been a busy weekend, to say the least."

Her hands freeze, and she looks up. "Are you screwing with me?"

"I feel like you should be saying something more romantic to me right now," I say, disentangling one of her hands so I can twine my fingers with hers. "Weren't you just telling me something about being in love with me? Something more like that."

"I am," she says softly. "So fucking in love with you."

"Yeah, I know the feeling." I rise onto my toes and press my lips to hers, and bozhe moi it feels like coming home. It's like our last night together all over again. I'm free and open to show her exactly how I feel, and I can't believe how long it took us to get back here. But we're here, and we're kissing, and—

There's a loud cough in my ear, and I step back to see Beth giving me a Look. "Not to interrupt your moment," she says wryly, "but there's a huge line waiting to get books signed, and while I'm sure they're all grateful for the demonstration of Happily Ever After, you *did* beg to work this event, and the part where people spend money is not quite over." She holds out a pad of sticky notes and a permanent marker, and I sheepishly take them. I'm about to apologize when she turns to Jasmine and holds out a hand. "I'm Beth. I imagine I'll be seeing you around."

Jasmine honest-to-goodness blushes. She is so damn cute. "I hope so," she says, cutting a look to me.

I wink and force myself toward the line.

When I'm done taking names and sticking them into books, I rejoin Jasmine by the counter and pull her to the side for a little more privacy. "So, to be clear, we're doing this thing. Right?"

She smirks. "Yes, Tinkerbell. We're doing this thing."

"You know your parents know."

"Oh, I know."

"Am I ever gonna be invited to sleep over again?"

"If you think I asked either of my parents that, you are out of your damn mind."

"I *am* out of my damn mind," I say, fiddling with her bracelets. "I dumped the most popular guy in school and tomorrow everyone's gonna know it's because I'm—I don't know what I am." I look at her. "Is that okay? That I don't know? It's just—there hasn't been another girl, ever. I don't know if I'm bi or if it's just you or if there's even a difference, but I don't really want to own a label until I know."

"No labels at all?" she asks, arching one of her thick, perfect brows. "How about 'girlfriend'?"

Girlfriend. It feels so different in Jasmine's voice than in Chase's, and it ripples down to my toes. "I can work with 'girlfriend.'"

"Good." She cups my face in her hands and kisses me. "Now take me to that graphic novel section you so carefully crafted and tell me more about this hot roommate character."

"You sure you want me to spoil the ending?" I ask as I lead her to a more private spot to, uh, definitely look at books and nothing else.

Her palm is exquisitely warm as it squeezes mine. "I think we've both waited long enough to turn the page in this story, don't you?"

Acknowledgments

All books are a challenge in their own way, but if I'm being honest, this one was the closest thing to an easy ride I've ever had, and that's unquestionably due to all the people I had in my corner for it.

To my editor, Vicki Lame, thank you for your keen editorial eye and every minute of seeing this book through. Big thanks also to Jennie Conway for your incredible work, kindness, and enthusiasm; Angelica Chong for your greatly appreciated assistance; my dream of a publicist, Meghan Harrington; designer Kerri Resnick and illustrator Claire Allison for an absolutely killer biconic cover; production pros Lauren Hougen, Cathy Turiano, and Anna Gorovoy for getting this book into tip-top shape; the fabulous marketing team of Alexis Neuville, DJ DeSmyter, and Brant Janeway, and everyone involved in Creative Services, Sales, and the School & Library teams for all your magic in spreading the word. It's no small task to get this all done during a global pandemic, and I couldn't have asked for a better place to do it.

To DongWon Song, thank you for loving this book the way it was and still pushing me to make it better in the best ways before finding it the perfect home.

To my agent, Patricia Nelson, thank you for holding my hand all the way down.

To the brilliant author friends I'm so lucky to have had as my earliest readers from first book to ninth, Marieke Nijkamp and Maggie Hall—I don't know how I would function in this world without you. You are both so brilliant and talented and make everything I do better and I love you gross amounts. And to Katherine Locke, thank you for walking me through every step of every dramatic turn of my life and career; if only you would alphabetize your bookcases you would be perfect.

Thank you to Anna-Marie McLemore for your early read and for your friendship in general—we'll always have Kalinda. Immeasurable thanks, too, to everyone who gave notes that helped make this book the best version of itself, including Katelyn Detweiler, Allie Levick, and especially Sari Fallas Linder, who let this very Ashkenazi author pick her beautiful Syrian brain.

I'm grateful to Jenn Marie Thorne, AK Furukawa, and Cam Montgomery for letting me throw my manuscript at them before I was ready to let it out into the world. Thank you to Becky Albertalli for all your support, always, and texts that keep me sane. I'm so grateful to her, Aminah Mae Safi, Jennifer Dugan, and Jen Wilde for the kind words on this book in particular and for dazzling my bookshelves in general.

Much love to all the friends who are there for me ad nauseum whether about publishing, parenting, or life in general, including but not limited to Emery Lord, Rick Lipman, Becca Podos, Eric Smith, Patrice Caldwell, Lev Rosen, Sona Charaipotra, Tess Sharpe, Jess Capelle, Sharon Morse, and the best digital quarantine-group buddies I could've asked for, Kind of a Big Deal [eggplant emoji] and "BFFs" Barrie, Liz, and Sasha.

Love to all my fellow book bloggers/media out there, especially those like Danika Leigh Ellis, YA Pride, the Lesbrary, and Tirzah Price, who do the work to help queer readers find the books that might fall through the cracks. Special shoutout to both Buzzfeed's YA team of Zoraida Córdova, Rachel Strolle, and our leader, Farrah Penn, and the people who've helped me keep LGBTQ Reads together this past year, including Rachel, Mark O'Brien, Shauna Morgan, and all the generous donors and patrons.

Deep gratitude to various other contributors to the writing of this book, especially the makers of Evernote, the Foo Fighters for "The Sky Is a Neighborhood," the Hilton Garden Inn Outer Banks/Kitty Hawk, Cheez-Its (especially whoever came up with kosher bacon-flavored ones), and, of course, Demi Lovato, whose strength and openness constantly awe me.

Most of all, thanks and love to my Adler and Fisch families. I am the luckiest wife, mom, daughter, sister, and aunt in the world, and I am so grateful for everything you make possible.